THE STORY OF PEACE

Miriam Ezeh

Published by
Bezalel Books
www.BezalelBooks.com
Waterford, MI

Printed in the United States of America

ISBN 978-0-9792258-1-9
Library of Congress 2007922537

Thank You, dearest Jesus, for Your Divine Mercy. To my dear husband, Ifeanyi, and everyone in the family, thank you for all your feedback, prayers, and support. Special thanks to Eby and Ik for your hard work in putting the cover together. To Cheryl, thank you for your patience throughout this process. To all who read this book, please accept my sincere gratitude. May God bless you abundantly.

Stacey,

Thank you so much for your interest in this book.

I hope you enjoy reading it.

May God Bless you.

With Gratitude,

Miriam

Aug 2007

CHAPTER 1

In a small farming village off the coast of Africa, the clouds displayed the golden brown effects of the sinking sun signaling the end of another work day. The occasional crows and bleats of animals surfaced amidst the laughter of children as they played in their parents' yards. The little ones had been to school, they had completed the day's chores, and now they remained outdoors determined to enjoy every remaining moment of the fading daylight. Farmers trekked home after another day of plowing the harsh soils while their wives prepared the modest meals that they would later call dinner. And for those women who opted to cook outside the house, the aroma of their meals mingled with the scent of wood smoke did not go unnoticed by any passerby.

In the southern end of this settlement sat a two story cement house. The structure, though quite small and unpainted, served its farming owners well. The main level consisted of a compact living room and a scant kitchen. On the upper level, the only bathroom in the house stood sandwiched between two bedrooms. The builder saw fit to roof the house with corrugated iron while the floors received nothing but a slab of concrete.

Laughter was once a common occurrence in this home. But a tragic event befell the inhabitants slashing their number from four to two. The lives and hearts of the surviving orphans propelled in opposite directions. And instead of laughter, the grey walls of the structure became witness to tears and arguments.

On this fine day, just as the other citizens of the village were sitting down to dinner in their homes, these two orphans sat in the kitchen of their unpainted cement farm house and engaged in a debate that would determine the outcome of their lives.

"Enough of these talks Lawrence! I can't stand it anymore!"

Lawrence shot up from our square wooden table and threw his long arms in the air. I knew he was frustrated, but there was no way I could ever accept his intentions. He strode to the window and observed the grazing animals while I buried my face in my hands. For what seemed like an eternity the only sound between us came from the goats outside. My teary gaze followed him to the window.

The bright light that once illumed our home had vanished for the day. Without a word I moved from the table just a few inches to the sink. My right hand reached beneath the aluminum sink for our kerosene lamp. I listened to my brother's slippered feet shuffling against the concrete floor as he turned away from his gaze. He watched in silent discomfort as I reached for a matchbox and performed the daily act of lighting the lamp. Within minutes a lone flame produced the faint glow that was to be our guide for the night.

Ignoring the shadows that appeared on our kitchen floor, I set the burning lamp on the table and reclaimed my spot on the bench. My gaze lingered absentmindedly on the lantern, our only source of light. Ever since the war, three years previous, electricity had not been supplied to our village. Those who could afford it purchased generators but with only three petrol stations within our reach, people used the gas guzzling machines for no more than three hours per night.

For me, the lack of power was one of the many reminders of the past violence. As I remembered the many lives that were lost, I could not understand why on earth my brother would take the position that he had just revealed to me.

Lawrence joined me at the table. With his calloused hands he held both my hands.

"My dear sister," he began. "There is no other way. We must fight to protect our land. Our enemies have already seized some property along the border. If we don't act right now our village will pay just like the last time."

His fiery eyes, affirming his determination, broke my heart. "How do you think you can fight the Se People? There are thousands of them, besides it's not worth the bloodshed."

Lawrence released my hands. "What do you suggest then?" He struggled to keep from yelling.

"Let's leave this place."

"And go where?"

"I don't know. We'll migrate somewhere and start over." Even as I spoke I knew my reply did not present much of a solution.

He rose again and began to pace the room.

"That's your reaction for everything, always run, run, and run! Achugoa says we have a chance. Don't you want to protect what's yours?"

I stood up and placed my hands on his lean shoulders. He stiffened at my touch.

"We've already lost mama and papa to warfare. I don't want to lose the only living relative I have left." I looked up at him, my eyes pleading. "You are only sixteen."

He brushed my hands away and stepped back, his youthful features contracting to reveal his irritation. "Have you forgotten how our ancestors came to settle on this land? Foreigners drove them away from their homes. When they arrived here it was nothing but elephant grass!" Bringing his hands before my face he bellowed, "They built this village with their bare hands! And you want to just give it up and run! What an insult to them!"

With my head shaking I answered, "I haven't forgotten, and I will never forget. But...." Before I could finish he marched out of the room. The back door slammed shut. He was gone again to one of those meetings organized by people who did not want peace.

Tears streamed down my cheeks at the memory of the previous conflict when our parents died. So much blood was shed over things, perishable things that were of no use in the next life. I loved our home just as much as my brother did. I loved our little house and our community in this village. Our roads were not paved like the city roads. We did not always have running water, but this was our home and I loved it. Even still, there was nothing more horrifying to me than the bloodshed threatening to break out once again.

In the same village, John Williams stood at the center of his potential home site and surveyed the area. At that moment, it was just an acre of grassland, but he knew where the two story house would stand. He envisioned a generously sized porch for relaxation and a stand alone garage a few feet from the left of the house. With the back of his hand, he wiped the sweat from his brow. He figured the temperature had to be at least 30 degrees Celsius. With one hand capped over his clean-shaven face he surveyed the land once more, his brain reminding him to quench his thirst.

The construction budget needed an adjustment to accommodate a borehole. Even at the age of twenty eight John knew he did not want to spend his energy walking miles just for a bucket of water. He would rather go running, do some push ups; anything but fetch water. He admired the patience and skill of the locals he saw in the mornings. They were mostly women, from seven to seventy, trudging through the dirt roads to the stream and returning home with the full buckets on their heads without any threat of the contained liquid spilling over.

Two agama lizards darted by, causing him to jump. John's gaze followed the eight inch reptiles as they disappeared among the grasses. The animals chased each other in a fashion that made him think of the grey squirrels in his birth country. He inhaled from the air surrounding him, his senses relishing that scent unique to greens. A deep feeling of gratitude filled the man at the thought that his dream would soon be realized. This was where he belonged. These were his people. They had a great need. In addition, he felt a deep calling to help.

This was his second time visiting this settlement. The first was just five years ago at his mother's passing. Her wish was to be buried in her place of birth, a land unknown to him. The first time he set foot on its hilly grounds, he was filled with intrigue at the *lifestyle of the locals. It was a lifestyle of simplicity and contentment and he knew right then that someday he would be back for good.*

It took a great deal of frugal living, but he had finally saved up enough money to make the move to this secluded part of the earth and build his own house. Now if only he had a wife. Being a handsome doctor made him a target for several women. But he had still yet to find the woman who would captivate his heart; a woman whose values mirrored his, a woman who would willingly reject the conveniences of city living for a life of less glamour.

With the sun beating down at maximum strength, he decided to head back to his relatives' home. As his jeep moved through the dirt roads John spied a slender figure in the distance carrying a basket on her head just like the local market women often did. At first he thought nothing of the sight and he would have driven past her but the fatigue in her movement caused him to decelerate his car. Her steps grew sluggish and eventually she stopped and moved the burden from her head unto the ground. With the intensity of the sun, he feared dehydration. He pulled up next to the woman with short braided hair. She was rubbing her forehead.

"Excuse me," he called. "Are you alright?" The startled woman lifted her face to reveal her striking beauty. Two almond shaped eyes stared back at him in uncertainty. Her dark brown skin could have easily been

likened to silk. The woman glanced back at her burden, then at the distance ahead. Her head pounded like drums and her muscles felt sore from all the day's lifting. But she could never ignore her mother's stern warnings never to get into a stranger's car. This man was not a domestic stranger. He also spoke with a foreign accent. With her mind made up, she turned to him and shook her head. Without waiting for another word from the man, she picked up her burden and moved away in haste.

CHAPTER 2

Sunday has always been a special day for me. When I was the only child my mother would carry me on her back and together with my father they would walk for an hour to Saint Mary's Catholic Church in the village center. Our walks were usually quiet, except for the sweet humming from my mother which I enjoyed so much. Even though I did not know the songs her melodic voice always gave me a sense of calm. Despite the long journey we always arrived a half hour early for mass.

Mother said the church was built in the early forties, by missionaries, before she was born. The forty foot cement building was painted white on the outside and on the inside I never tired of beholding the huge crucifix that suspended from the ceiling above the altar. A candle encased in a red lantern burned at the altar. Later, I understood its significance in making us aware of the real presence of our Lord Jesus in the Tabernacle.

Upon entering the church we would always genuflect, all three of us. Mother would whisper to me once we settled in the pews.

"Tell Jesus anything that you wish to share with Him. He loves you so much and He is listening to you." The first time she said these words, I stared at her speechlessly. Nothing seemed to come to mind.

"Go ahead," she coaxed with a smile. "Tell Him about your morning." So I closed my eyes and whispered to the almighty God what I had for breakfast.

As time passed, I grew accustomed to this practice and mother did not have to remind me anymore. I looked forward to the time when I would talk with Jesus alone. Oftentimes I would share the details of my day with Him including the happy moments and the not so happy moments. Other times I would ask Him for guidance on a problem that I encountered. Or I would just sit quietly before Him, listening to anything He may want to tell me. I knew that He always listened and sometimes I would hear Him speak to me in those quiet moments.

Introducing me to Jesus was the best thing my mother did for me. It was infinitely more valuable than any monetary inheritance. When she and Papa died, I turned to my Savior with my pain. Lawrence and I were all alone except, of course, for Christ. It is clear to me now how He knew our needs because just when it seemed like our future was hopeless the Lord brought Mr. and Mrs. Ebem into our lives.

The memory of my first meeting with Mrs. Ebem has remained fresh in my mind even after three years. After the funeral, I found myself following the grassy path that led back to the church from the cemetery. The humidity brought forth beads of sweat on my forehead. Despite the napkin in my possession, I did not bother to wipe my face. In the distance I heard my brother calling to me.

"Where are you going?" he had asked. "That's not the way home."

I did not turn to look at him. "I'm going back to the church for a moment. "I'll meet you at home," I answered. The sound of his footsteps faded away as I continued to the church. In less than five minutes I passed through the side double doors into the silent presence of God. The only source of light came from the lantern at the altar. My footsteps echoed throughout the building as I made my way to the front of the church. Facing the Tabernacle, both of my knees came down in genuflection. With my hands clasped before me, I cleared my throat and took a quick glance over my shoulder. My brief scan did not detect any other worshiper. *There is no one here besides me and Jesus.* I felt comfortable praying aloud.

"My dear Jesus, it's me." The tears that gathered in my eyes spilled onto my cheeks. My heart had never known such grief as it did at that moment. But despite the circumstance I took comfort in the fact that the Lord would never leave us. With my napkin I wiped my cheek. "My mother and father are gone," I continued in my stricken voice. "Please accept them into Your kingdom. They really did try their best while they were here with us." I paused to blow into my napkin before offering more prayers for my parents.

"I don't know what will happen to Lawrence and me," I continued. "Lord You know how much we have left and You alone know how much we really need. I just entrust everything into Your hands. I abandon our lives and our home into Your hands. Please give us the Grace to work hard and to persevere. It will not be easy, but the Angel Gabriel told our Blessed Mother that nothing is impossible with You, dear God. Therefore, I will go home in confidence, trusting in Your Divine will, and asking that we may never do anything to separate ourselves from You, dearest Jesus."

As I rose to my feet I felt the sense of relief that I always felt after leaving things in the Hands of God. I genuflected one last time before making my way through the side doors and into the sunlight. I was only half way through the parking grounds when a woman called out my name. I turned around to behold her plumpish figure standing at the church steps. The look of empathy in her face gave me the notion that she may have been inside the church the whole time. I retraced my steps back to where she stood. She introduced herself, even though it was not necessary.

Nobody was richer than Mr. and Mrs. Ebem in our village of eight thousand. They stood out because they were not farmers. They were entrepreneurs who, after years of running successful restaurants in several cities, decided to leave the businesses in the hands of their capable sons and retire in the village. Most people already knew them for their kindness toward orphans. They commanded the respect of the villagers. And even the village chiefs would occasionally seek their advice.

Not only did Mrs. Ebem offer to pay our school fees, but she also wanted to replace the money that we had spent on our parents' funerals. *Dear Jesus I thank You.* As I stood listening to the kind woman, I repeated the simple prayer over and over in my heart.

I brought up the topic of paying Mrs. Ebem back but she rebuked me. She almost seemed offended as she spoke the words, "My child, do not worry about that. Accept the favor and be the best you can be." It was then that I understood her reasoning. She did not want monetary payback. She wanted to see us become good hardworking citizens, conscientious and faithful to God. That would be her reward. And I hoped that she would one day live to see her dreams for us become a reality.

One Sunday after mass, many months later, I spotted Mr. and Mrs. Ebem outside the church. The sun withdrew behind the clouds allowing us to enjoy the cool breeze that caressed our skins. For a moment I stood and watched the couple. With arms interlocked, they sauntered to their white Mercedes which sat at the center of the grassy parking lot. My heart filled with gratitude and I hurried across the grounds to greet them. Mr. Ebem was the first to spot my approach.

"Our beautiful daughter is here," he said to his wife. She adjusted the gold-framed glasses on her rounded face. It seemed like that little gesture made all the difference for her eyes lit up at once as she extended her arms for an embrace. For a brief moment, I disappeared into her kind arms, the sharp scent of her foreign perfume tickling at my nasal senses. I rubbed my nose to keep from sneezing.

"How are you doing dear?" asked the motherly woman.

"Very well thank you ma." Through her lens she studied my face. I fiddled with my black veil draped over my braids.

"You look well enough," concluded the woman. I breathed a sigh of relief.

Then glancing around the lot, she asked, "Where is that brother of yours? We haven't seen much of him these days." I scanned the lot myself but to no avail.

I returned my gaze to the woman, "We came here together."

Mr. Ebem thumbed his grey beard. The fine line on his forehead deepened with concern. "There seems to be tension along the border with the Ses." He shook his head as though he had just announced the news of a death. "It's a pity." With his brows wrinkled in deep thoughts, I sensed that something else troubled him.

"I say we just build a wall to mark the border and end all this confusion," added Mrs. Ebem, who had also observed her husband.

The man grunted. "My dear, I wish it were that easy." Suddenly he turned to me. "What do you think Peace?" I thought for a moment. I would have answered, but the sight of a stranger took me by surprise.

The tall man emerged from the church and approached us. As he took confident strides in our direction, I knew for sure that he was the same stranger that had offered to help me the previous week on my way to the market.

Again, Mr. Ebem caught sight of the man before his wife. "There you are! I was beginning to wonder if you'd left already."

At these words his wife adjusted her glasses and glanced over her shoulder. "Oh no not John," she corrected, her head shaking vigorously. "You can count on John to stay behind after mass." Politely ignoring the couple's chatter, the stranger fixed an earnest gaze on me and nodded in greeting.

Before I could react, Mrs. Ebem grabbed my arm and moved me closer to her robust frame. "Allow me to introduce the beautiful Peace Udomm," she said to the stranger.

He held out his hand. "John Williams." And with a smile he added, "You look a lot stronger today." My gaze shifted to the married couple. I expected that at least one of them would have liked to know what John meant by his last statement. Had we met before? Where or when did our meeting take place? To my surprise they both seemed satisfied with the present circumstance.

"John is visiting from the States," added Mrs. Ebem. *That explains the accent.* For an awkward moment no one spoke. I saw Mrs. Ebem deliver a gentle jab of her elbow to her husband's side.

Taking the cue from his wife, he cleared his throat. "I'm afraid our aged legs cannot hold us up for too long. We'll be on our way." With that the couple ambled away leaving John and me alone. I knew he wanted to make eye contact but I did not feel up to the challenge. Instead, I fixed my gaze on a nearby bush.

"Perhaps you would allow me to drive you home. Now that we've been introduced, I'm no longer a stranger." Even his gentle tone could not encourage me to accept the offer.

My eyes resumed a vain search for Lawrence. "Thank you, but my brother and I usually walk home together." I left him at once.

"It's almost midnight where have you been?" Lawrence shut the door behind his lanky body and walked past me, ignoring my question.

I rose from the bench and followed him. "Answer me!"

He stopped just before our narrow stairs. "Unlike some people, I spent the day figuring out how to defend our home." His words pierced like a thorn but I maintained my composure.

"Do you realize how worried I've been? Please tell me you didn't go to Achugoa's meeting."

He looked away, his silence betraying his actions.

"What did he tell you this time?"

His frown hardened at the question.

"So now you are involved in secrecy?"

"I can't talk."

A destabilizing chill ran up my spine compelling me to lean against the cold, hard wall for support. My brother was keeping secrets with men who embraced violence as the solution to our troubles. I looked up at him.

"Please stop this," I begged. "Why are you doing this?"

Lawrence's gaze went straight into my eyes. "You wouldn't understand." His low tone was loaded with resolve. He turned his back toward me. With an aching heart I left the stairs and returned to the kitchen.

Without electricity our miniature refrigerator was useless. So I took my brother's untouched dinner and fed it to the goats. I then retreated to my bedroom, but sleep did not come. My brother was headed for trouble and I could not stop him. With our parents gone, it was my mission to care for the boy for as long as I lived. I rose every morning and prepared breakfast just like mother used to do. I saw him off to school, helped him with his homework, prepared dinner, did our laundry, cleaned the house, mended our clothes, went to the market, and performed some of the farm chores. I even turned down the Ebem's offer to send me to college in the city. I did this all with no thought of myself. Feeling like I did, it was easy for me to embrace the truth that Jesus has an immeasurable love for each one of us because my love for my brother was immense.

Before long I heard his cries coming from the other bedroom. It was not the first time Lawrence spent his night in tears. If only he would let me share in his grief. The day before, I entered his room at the sound of his weeping but he begged me to leave. Why did he keep pushing me away? Why was he choosing to travel down this destructive path? His muffled cries brought hot tears to my eyes.

My dream was to see Lawrence happily settled as a grown up. But with Achugoa preying on our youth, I did not know what would become of the boy. What was I to do? Perhaps the Ebems may be able to get through to him. At that moment, I made a decision to pay them a visit as soon as possible.   I then knelt before my bed and prayed for my brother.

CHAPTER 3

The following afternoon, I passed through the iron gates of the Ebem's residence. The sight of that black jeep wrangler parked in one of the garages brought me to a halt. My heart rate doubled, but why? Why should the presence of John Williams have any effect on me? Composing myself, I walked past the marigold bushes to the intricately carved double doors. I took one last calming breath as my index finger pushed on the doorbell.

The wooden piece of art opened to reveal the young man dressed in jeans and a white cotton shirt. "Peace! What a pleasant surprise! Come in."

I crossed the threshold, my palms growing moist. "Good evening Mr. Williams."

"Mr. Williams?" He uttered his own name as though the words left a bitter taste in his mouth. "John will be just fine," he continued with a smile. I'm not very good with civilities." He led me through the two story entrance to the living room and offered me a seat while he remained standing. "I assume you want to see my aunt." He must have read the question in my face because he went on to explain, "My late mother is Mr. Ebem's sister."

His mother had passed away. I could not help but to empathize with him on his loss.

"You've lost your mother. I'm sorry."

John appeared moved by my statement but he did not acknowledge it. As I waited to hear what traveled through his mind, the facial similarities he shared with his uncle became obvious. Both men had the same brownish mahogany skin, narrowed eyes and masculine jaw. But unlike his uncle's bearded jaw, John's youthful face looked like he had never gone a day without shaving.

He took a few steps to the leather chair adjacent to mine and settled into it, his expression solemn. "My aunt tells me you've lost your parents. I can only imagine how hard it must have been. You and your brother have worked really hard to stay together and to keep your household going. You have my admiration for that."

"Thank you. Jesus has really taken care of us and He continues to do so."

His features produced a smile. "I understand what you mean."

A moment of silence passed between us. Not daring to prolong the conversation any longer, I clasped my palms together, which seemed to grow sweatier by the minute, and sealed my lips shut.

"Well," he began, rising to his feet, "I'll let them know you are here." With that he left the room while I scolded myself for getting so nervous.

For thirty minutes I sat alone in Mr. and Mrs. Ebem's leather chair and considered the best way to break the disappointing news to them. They had such high hopes for Lawrence. When my brother finished first in his class last year, the Ebems were so pleased that they began to encourage him to think about what he might want to study in college.

I was still rehearsing the words when Mrs. Ebem came down the large spiral stairway. As usual she donned a gown colorful enough to compete with her pet peacocks in the backyard. The woman sunk into the leather armchair to my left.

"Sorry for the delay," she began. "My husband and I were on the phone trying to convince the village chiefs to negotiate with the Se people."

Mrs. Ebem picked up her feather fan and began to cool herself. "It must be very hot outside. Would you like the maid to get you a drink?"

"No ma. I've come to ask a favor."

A compassionate smile shone in her face. "Dear child, what can we do for you?"

"It's about Lawrence."

"Is he well?" was her concerned response.

"Yes he is." My voice began to tremble. "But he has gotten involved with Achugoa." At the mention of that name the woman stopped fanning herself. I went on to tell her about my brother's meetings with Achugoa, his resolution to fight, and the secrecy in which he was involved. At the end of it all, she placed one bejeweled hand on my shoulder.

"Don't worry my child. We will speak to him."

With a sense of relief, I rose to leave. "Thank you so much ma." She nodded in acknowledgement then called out her nephew's name. The composed man appeared at the living room entrance.

"John, why don't you drive Peace home?" She suggested with a wave of her hand.

He turned his gaze in my direction. "I would be honored to."

"No, thank you," I said as politely as I could. "It's only a thirty minute stroll. I can walk."

"Oh no!" countered the mistress of the house. "I won't allow you to walk when transportation is available. I'm sure you have things to do when you get home. Save your energy for your chores."

In silence, John and I left the house and headed for his jeep. To my surprise, he came around to the passenger side and opened the door for me. I stood my ground, a little unsure of what to do next. A smile formed across his face.

"Go ahead, get in." He motioned with his hand. Without another word I stepped into the car while simultaneously struggling to hide my disconcertion. No one had ever held a door for me before. It is not that I was unaware of this gesture. Often times I had seen the Ebem's driver open doors for his employers. As far as I was concerned, it was something that only the wealthy could experience from their servants.

During the drive home, John started to speak in our native tongue. "I couldn't help overhearing some of the conversation about your brother," he said. Don't hesitate to let me know if there is anything I can do to help."

I remained speechless for I didn't know whether to ask him if he was eaves dropping, to thank the man for his offer, or to comment on the fluency with which he spoke. When he spoke in English he sounded quite unlike us, yet when he spoke in the native tongue one would never guess that he knew any other language.

With a chuckle he continued, "I get that silent reaction all the time around here. You did not think I could speak my mother's language, did you?"

The seconds that passed allowed me to recover from the surprise. "You're very fluent."

"Thanks to my mom," he returned. "Growing up she wouldn't let me speak English in the house." I began to consider how much discipline it must have required on his mother's part to raise a bilingual child. My thoughts did not get very far because John interrupted with a question.

"My aunt tells me you have spent all your twenty one years in this village?"

"Yes." Even as I answered a part of me felt surprised that such a conversation would even transpire between John and Mrs. Ebem.

With his eyes on the road he sought to know more. "Do you ever wish to see the outside world?"

Without giving it a bit of thought I answered, "I like it here."

My answer brought a smile to his face. "Me too, it has been my intention to settle down here for good...open up a clinic and hopefully grow it into a hospital."

"You must be a doctor."

He nodded then continued. "The nearest hospital is an hour's drive away. That's not very comforting, especially in emergency situations. I heard so many died in the last war because they lacked access to medical treatment. A clinic would do some good I'm sure. What do you think?"

I could not bring myself to answer him. I looked away as the tears gathered in my eyes. Without meaning to, John had taken me back to that awful day three years ago, the day that marked the first day of the previous conflict. Prior to that day the conflict had not become a reality yet. There were rumors, but like other villagers, we did not expect anything to come out of it. As a result, we tried our best to carry on with our daily lives.

Our family had such an excess of produce that year that our parents enlisted our help to take all the fruits to the market. Lawrence and I needed to be in school by nine o'clock in the morning. On that fateful day we rose very early, before the sun even made known its presence, and dressed in our school uniforms. For me, it was a white buttoned shirt and a green drawstring skirt that came down to my shins. For Lawrence it was a white shirt as well, but with green shorts.

Papa pushed a wheel barrow of yams. Lawrence pushed another barrow filled with mangoes. Mama and I trailed behind with our baskets resting on our heads. We trekked in silence except for the occasional interruption of a dog's bark or the greeting of a rooster.

Daylight was in full swing when we reached the market. We walked through the arched entryway. As we passed the first stall, my parents exchanged greetings with Mr. Okin the clothing trader. Most villagers bought attires from him. His wife and their five daughters did all the sewing while he took on the role of selling them for the best possible price. That morning the balding, lean man worked to unload his merchandise from the trunk of his battered 504 Peugeot. We walked on, exchanging greetings with other early starters until we arrived at my parents' stall.

"Now go off you two," began my mother. "We don't want you to be late for school." My brother and I did not protest. We exchanged goodbyes and left our parents to set up for the day.

We had only walked a few feet from the market entrance when a thundering sound shook the earth. We each stumbled but did not lose our balance. Suddenly, the temperature shot up by what felt like one hundred degrees. Then I saw smoke, thick black smoke floating up to the sky from the market. Lawrence and I exchanged stunned glances. Without a word we both raced back to the market entrance. I saw flames, unrelenting flames consuming everything in its path. Then Mr. Okin, with the help of two others emerged through the entrance. They were carrying my parents' unconscious bodies to his car.

"What's wrong?" John's voice, laden with concern, snapped me out of my reverie. I let out a pained sigh. While John waited for my answer, about twenty cows driven by a team of cattle herders emerged from the left side of the road. John had no choice but to step on his brakes so that the cows could make their way across the dirt passage.

When he looked at me, I quickly wiped the tears from the corners of my eyes. Immediately he shifted the gear to reverse and carefully backed a few feet away to allow ample space for the approaching animals.

Then giving me his full attention he asked, "Peace, you're crying. What's wrong?"

I could not speak right away. Animal sounds coupled with the voices of cattle herders filled the air. The deep mooing from the cows lasted for full minute before ceasing momentarily.

In the midst of the short lull I answered, "My parents, after they were injured we tried to get them to the hospital but they died on the way. The hospital was too far."

He sat, speechless. His eyes revealed the sorrow he felt for awakening my pain.

"I'm sorry." The earnest nature of his tone moved me.

Hoping to ease John's guilt I struggled to produce a smile, "It's not your fault."

The deep sounds from the animals intensified once more, forcing us to wait in silence until the last cow was safely off the road.

As soon as we could hear each other again, I turned to John. "Please take me home." With a nod he started the engine and resumed our short journey.

Later that night I barely slept. I thought about my parents' killers. We never found out their individual identities. We only know they came from the Se village. I had already forgiven them but I wondered, for their sakes and for the sakes of others, if they ever repented of their actions. Mother always used to say that there was nothing worse than the refusal of a sinner to repent. So I knelt by my bed and prayed once again that, if they had not already done so, they would approach the merciful God and seek forgiveness.

The following afternoon I used our kerosene stove to prepare some goat soup for Lawrence and me. As I worked in solitude I wondered if he would be home on time. The meal had just come to a boil when loud knocks sounded against the front door.

Before I opened the door I peered through the hole. John stood patiently beside his uncle. Without a moment's hesitation, I turned the locks. His uncle donned his usual traditional attire, cotton textile pants and a long shirt that came all the way down to his knees despite his oversized midsection. John dressed in a white shirt and blue jeans. Both men wore sandals.

"Welcome," I greeted as I stepped aside to let them in. The older man entered first and occupied one of the two benches in the living room. John settled into the adjacent one.

Mr. Ebem went straight to the point. "Where is he?

I understood the reason for his visit. "Lawrence is not back yet."

The man glanced at his silver watch, his brows exposing his puzzlement. "Ah! School let out two hours ago."

I nodded. "It's been like this for a while. Is this a phase he will out grow?" My question went unanswered as Papa Ebem consulted his watch again.

"Let's wait a bit," suggested John, who was silent until then.

Without thinking I did what my mother taught me by her example. She never let a guest leave our house on an empty stomach.

"I will bring you some soup."

The men exchanged knowing glances.

"Who can resist that aroma?" began Mr. Ebem, "I'm sure John will be glad to taste your cooking."

My eyes darted in John's direction. He made no effort to dispute his uncle's comment.

CHAPTER 4

While the men ate, we spent the next hour in general conversation. With their meals finished, I rose and gathered their bowls to the kitchen. As I washed the dishes, the sound of the men speaking in hushed tones reached my ears. I could not make out their exact words, neither did I attempt to. I dried my hands on a dishrag and returned to the living room.

Mr. Ebem spoke as soon as I returned from the kitchen, "Daughter, how are things going with your orchard?" I smiled at his concern. Every year he asked the same question to ensure that we could at least earn some money from the produce.

"Very well," I answered. "The fruits are sweet and the yield is much more than we expected. I thank God."

"That's great news," replied Mr. Ebem, his voice betraying his relief. "It's always good to have something to take to the market."

"Would you like a bag of mangoes to take home with you?"

Mr. Ebem hesitated at my offer. He started to shake his head, but I interrupted.

"It's no problem," I assured. "I can go to the orchard right now and harvest them for you."

"I know your days are filled with countless chores," replied the man. "Don't tack on another errand to your list on my account."

"Papa, it is the least I can do to show my gratitude for all the kindness you've bestowed on us."

At these words Mr. Ebem did not protest anymore. I rose to my feet. With my eyes on the fatherly man I concluded, "I'll try my best to be quick."

I turned to leave the room but John interrupted. "If you don't mind, I'll be glad to help?"

Mr. Ebem's face displayed a grin at the suggestion. "Good idea John," he said, turning to his nephew. "There is no need for Peace to do everything herself." Then returning his gaze to me he joked, "Make him carry the bag too."

Rising from the bench John joked along with his uncle, "Do you want to join us?" he asked, smiling.

Mr. Ebem let out one of his hearty chuckles. "You know the answer to that John. Asking me if I want to join you out there is like asking a tortoise if he wants to race. No thank you. Let me relax on the porch."

With my basket under my arm, we stepped down from the porch into the sunlight. It took my eyes a moment to adjust to the bright rays. I glanced up at John. He had already slipped on his sunglasses. As usual we were greeted by the goat's calls that came from the left side of the house. Ignoring the bleats of the animals, we turned east toward the orchard.

Suddenly feeling discomfort from the silence between us, I began to speak, "The orchard is my favorite part of the farm."

"Why?"

"It is mostly quiet. And when the birds sing, it is relaxing. The trees provide a cool shade from the sun and oftentimes I prefer to sit under the trees during my break from the day's work."

"In other words, you love nature."

I thought for a while. "Now that you mention it, I do believe so. The house can never be as relaxing as it is out there."

"I can't wait to see it."

John and I continued up a sloped path. We passed a fenced off parcel on our right. It was only a tenth of an acre. I observed John's gaze linger on the weeds and grass that permeated the land but he said nothing. Instead he glanced back at his uncle still sitting on the porch.

When he was sure Mr. Ebem could not hear us John turned to me and asked, "Peace, you have been on my mind. Please do not think of me as forward but I need to know how you are doing." He made no effort to hide the care from his tone. Until then, I had been oblivious of how much my tears from yesterday troubled him. John possessed a kind of gentleness about him that made me want to tell him everything. I especially wanted to tell him how many times I stayed up late waiting up for my brother. But my lips would not speak the words. As nice as John was to me, I still did not feel like I knew him that well. Instead I bottled up my thoughts and twisted the lid shut.

With a feigned confidence I answered, "Don't worry about us. But thank you for asking. You are a kind man." He looked disappointed. I sensed he would have preferred a more honest, personal answer. He opened his mouth to say something but thought better of it. Instead he fell into an unexpected silence, like one in deep contemplation.

We followed a grassy path, populated with green grasshoppers, to the orchard where we stood side by side. "Mother used to take these to the market for sale," I said pointing to the mangoes that still hung from the trees.

He turned to me. "Is that what you were doing the first time I saw you?"

I placed my basket on the ground. "Yes."

"You were so exhausted," he recalled. "I thought you would faint for sure."

"I had a terrible headache."

"Why didn't you let me help you?"

"If you did turn out to be dangerous, and something happened to me, who would care for my brother?"

My remark brought a smile to his face. "Your brother is very blessed to have you."

With all seriousness, I shook my head at his compliment.

"Why, you don't think so?"

"Lawrence wouldn't have gotten involved with bad company if I had been more careful. It happened right under my nose and I didn't know about it till he started talking of going to fight."

He grimaced at my thinking. "Oh Peace, you've done a lot more than you think. My aunt has nothing but the very best things to say about you!"

When I failed to respond, he strolled a few feet away from me. This brought him under one of the trees. At first he showed little interest in the plant. But as I watched, his gaze focused on the roots and moved all the way up to the branches. With my hands in my dress pockets, I waited patiently. It would only be a matter of time before he asked a question.

"There are so many mangoes. How many trees are here?"

"About twenty"

"That's a lot of fruit. How do you get to reap them all?"

My face fell at his question. "We are not always able to complete the harvests on time."

"Hmmm," with his eyes still on the tree he digested my answer. I waited.

Then he asked, "What happens to the produce that you don't get to market?"

"The neighbors come by and help themselves."

He rolled up his sleeves. "In that case we better get started. I think we can knock out a couple of trees while we are here."

My jaw dropped in surprise as I stood, speechless. Surely he could not be serious.

He lowered his face to examine his shirt. "What's the problem? Is there a lizard on me or something?"

The humor in his face caused me to chuckle. "I appreciate the offer John, but I think we should just stick to retrieving a handful of mangoes for your uncle. Your white shirt would surely be ruined if you try to harvest more."

In that moment we witnessed the approach of a vehicle in the distance. I looked toward the house, and then I returned my gaze to John. His features no longer bore the traces of humor from a moment ago.

"We should go back." I said.

"Of course," he agreed. John grabbed my basket from the ground and led the way back.

Had the circumstances been different I would have stopped to marvel at the shades of purple and orange present in the sky. But a strange red pickup with about a dozen frowning boys seated in the back had just pulled up in front of our home. I recognized a few of them to be Lawrence's classmates. My brother emerged from the pack and hopped onto the ground, his sandaled feet stirring up some dust. The boys did not exchange words. With a wave of Lawrence's hand, the vehicle jolted away, leaving us in a cloud of dust. Lawrence started toward the house. But as soon as he spotted Mr. Ebem sitting on our front porch he stopped in his tracks and stared at me as though I had betrayed him. Papa Ebem introduced his nephew to my brother then we all entered the house.

Once everyone was seated, Papa Ebem wasted no time in getting down to business. "What is this I hear about you wanting to fight?" he asked to Lawrence. With parted lips and both palms opened toward the ceiling, my brother sent me a questioning scowl which did not escape Mr. Ebem's attention.

"Yes Peace told us all about it because she cares about you," he continued. "It is the same concern for you that has brought me here today." The boy folded his long arms and sealed his lips shut. "What do you have to say for yourself?" Mr. Ebem pushed on.

Lawrence leaned forward in his woven chair. "I want to fight. I am not ashamed of it."

Mr. Ebem's face saddened at the news. "Do you think your parents would like that for you if they were here today?"

The teenager raised his shoulders nonchalantly.

Mr. Ebem's face took on an intense seriousness. "You must disassociate yourself from Achugoa! Is that clear?"

Lawrence could not stand those instructions. "This is not right!" He jabbed a finger at me. Why must you take her side?"

"Because I did not spend the last three years paying your school fees so that you can go and have yourself killed! You have a bright future ahead of you. Why do you want to throw it all away?"

The boy shot up from his seat. "This is injustice!"

"Sit down!" ordered the older man. "What do you know about injustice?" Lawrence remained standing. "Sit down I said!" The thundering sound of the man's voice reverberated through the room causing my brother to obey reluctantly.

The elder man raised an index finger. "Listen to me attentively because I'm only going to say this once. Either you stop meeting with Achugoa or I stop paying your tuition. You decide."

Lawrence hesitated then answered. "I will stop meeting with Achugoa."

"Good," returned Ebem.

As I worked in the orchard the following afternoon my heart leapt for joy at the sight of Lawrence. *Thank goodness he came straight home from school.* He approached with a woven basket in one hand and our harvesting tool in the other. The homemade device consisted of a wooden pole, about six foot long with a blunt metal hook attached to one end. He strolled right past me and stopped under the tree next to the one that I was harvesting.

"How was school today?" I asked. He eyed me without a word. I knew he was sulking. I would give him some time. We worked in silence filling baskets with fruits for thirty minutes until he left for the house to get a drink of water.

Upon his return I tried again. "Did you see what I made for dinner?" When he refused to answer I continued, "Yam porridge, it's your favorite!"

The scowl he delivered dampened my mood. "Just leave me alone," he said.

But I could not comply with his request. "You're still upset about yesterday. Please understand. I did it for your own good."

He picked up the tool and reached for a greenish yellow mango. With a soft pull on the stem, the fruit separated from its branch and fell right into Lawrence's grip. His silent treatment got the better of me. Was he oblivious to how much pain he caused others by sulking?

"Lawrence!"

He let out a frustrated sigh. "Leave me alone. Find something else to obsess about. You can marry that John, or whatever his name is, for all I care. Just stay out of my business." He moved to place the healthy treat into his basket.

My brother's reference to John put me in a fluster. Suddenly the words of reprimand that filled my mind vanished without a trace. With my hands folded before me, I stammered, "Um, uh how did John come into this conversation?"

Without stopping his task Lawrence answered, "I may be sixteen but I am not blind. Did you not see his face when he said goodbye to you yesterday? And now he is waiting for you at the house."

I took several deep breaths to calm myself as I made my way back to the house to meet John. With his hands resting in his pockets, he leaned on his jeep. When he saw me his expression awakened. He shifted his full weight to his feet and awaited my approach. I clasped my hands to my face in surprise at his attire. He was dressed in the brown t-shirt and khaki overalls, an outfit which many in our village considered to be laborer's clothing.

"You look just like a farmer," I gasped.

"Yep," he returned. "I got it this morning at the market. Now you are gonna have to let me help out with the harvests."

Like a smitten schoolgirl, my heart continued its accelerated beating as we showed John how to pluck the mangoes. And after hours of serious labor we had baskets of juicy fruits to take to the market. When John left that night, his demeanor told of his exhaustion.

CHAPTER 5

By the time John's jeep passed through the gates of his uncle's residence, every muscle in his body protested in pain. After hours of harvesting mangoes he longed for a warm shower and his bed. He parked before one of the garages and exited the vehicle to be greeted by the clamor of the generator engine in the backyard. For a split second he observed the myriad of stars that filled the sky. "This is beautiful," he muttered to himself. But his legs threatened to give way. Too bad he could not stand much longer to admire the breathtaking sight above. Sluggish strides brought him to the carved double doors. As quietly as he could he turned the key and stepped into the foyer. His right hand reached for the wall and flipped the light switch. The chandelier above released an intense glow that lighted not just the foyer but the hallway leading to the kitchen. He thought about Peace and Lawrence sitting in their little house with that dim kerosene lamp. If only he could share this little convenience with them, even if it was just for an hour. He worried about their eye sights. How many more years of inadequate lighting could they take? With his mind still on the pair he took stealth steps to the kitchen fridge and helped himself to a cold glass of water.

When he emptied the glass, he found himself thinking about the amazing woman that lived in a farmhouse. Her staying power shocked him. John's muscles practically turned against him just after one day of farm work. Yet here was a woman who performed manual labor on a daily basis. How could she do all that work outside the house and still have the energy to complete the household chores? Lawrence did his part at the farm but even with the boy's help the work, in John's opinion, seemed too much for them. He reflected upon the fact that she had to do virtually every task the manual way. Running water had long ceased to be in existence, there were no washers, no dryers, no dishwashers, or blenders. To make things worse her brother had also become a source of heartache for her. And through it all she remained hospitable. Without a doubt he knew that God's grace sustained her. He closed his eyes and uttered a short prayer on her behalf.

"Thank You God for the amazing strength that You give her. May her faith in You grow even stronger with each day."

Afterwards John moved quietly up the stairs to the guest room. His uncle and aunt were early sleepers and early risers. Even though the living room clock had just struck eight, he perceived they were already fast asleep. He also knew that they would rise early enough to attend the six o'clock morning mass.

John turned the knob leading into his spacious room. The freshly made bed had never looked more inviting. But he needed to resist until after his shower. His skin felt sticky from the day's humidity. He padded across the terrazzo floor to turn on the air conditioning unit. Cool refreshing air rushed through the vents. He squatted so that the air could blow right into his face. The Ebem's housekeeper usually stopped the generator at eleven o'clock. A deep sense of gratitude permeated him at the thought of having three more hours of air conditioning for the night.

The doctor slept until late the next day. It was Wednesday morning, the special day for perpetual adoration at St. Mary's church. Before sunrise the movements of his hosts stirred him as they prepared for the six o'clock daily mass. A part of him wanted to rise and attend with them. But the weaker part of him interrupted, reminding him of how tired he felt and how much he needed to rest a little more. He lifted his eyelids. He should try to get up. After all he could always return after mass and catch up on his sleep. He made a feeble attempt at lifting a hand. But his whole body felt like lead. Before long his eyelids drooped to a close and he resumed his snoring until his aunt knocked on his door at eleven thirty in the morning.

Once the raps reached his ears, he opened his eyes and slowly brought himself to a seating position. *"Come in,"* he permitted in a ruffled voice.

Mrs. Ebem turned the knob and poked her head through the opening. *"Are you alright John? You've never slept this late. I just wanted to make sure you weren't coming down with something."*

He stifled a yawn. *"Nothing is wrong,"* he replied. *"I am just a little tired."*

"Tired from what? You don't have malaria do you?" The woman's voice carried a bit of concern. Not wishing to speak in his roughened voice, he shook his head. But his aunt displayed that look on her face which told him that she was not convinced.

"Trust me aunt Florence, I don't have malaria." The hoarseness still influenced John's voice. It did not matter to aunt Florence that her nephew was a doctor who had spent a considerable amount of time studying the illness.

"Then why did you sleep for so long?" she persisted.

He cleared his throat and decided to calm her concerns. *"I worked at a farm yesterday."*

With a bemused look she asked, *"What farm?"* Before he could answer she figured out the answer for herself. The new realization snatched the frown from her face and replaced it with a huge grin.

"That Peace, she's such a wonderful girl. I can see why you are drawn to her." With that she removed her head from the

opening and shut the door leaving her nephew alone.

John dressed quickly and drove to St. Mary's church. He knew he had already missed the morning masses, but he wanted to spend some time before God. He entered through the back door and genuflected. There were many others already kneeling in prayer.

Not wanting to be a source of distraction, he found a place in one of the back pews and knelt as well. There was something that he especially wanted to bring before the Lord that day, something to do with Peace. His aunt was right about one thing; no, two things. Peace was very special and he was drawn to her. But he needed to seek God's will on the matter. One thing was for sure. If Peace's vocation had to do with marriage, he hoped that the blessed man would treasure her, respect her dignity, and love her just as Christ loved the Church. As willing as he was to be that man, he was not sure that the Lord wanted for him to be that person. And so he prayed.

An hour later he stood outside, at the church steps. When his stomach growled he consulted his watch and was surprised to find that it was already two o'clock in the afternoon. Without a doubt his aunt must have saved some of her spicy cooking for him. He would have proceeded down the stairs to his vehicle, but the sight of that wonderful girl moving across the parking lot stopped him.

She looked so dignified in her traditional flowing dress and matching head tie accented with the light embroidery of some talented seamstress. She approached with her right hand in her pocket and her left hand supporting the small bag that hung from her shoulder.

He descended the stairs to meet her. "How are you?" he asked in earnest.

She offered a smile. "I'm well, thank you, and you?"

"I'm well too," he answered adopting her form of speech. "How is Lawrence?"

"He is at home studying. Thank you for asking."

"You're welcome."

His gaze moved past her as though he searched for something. Then turning to her he asked, "Did you walk all the way here?"

"Yes."

"Wow," was his amazed response. He thought about all the work she must have completed earlier in the day before taking the hour long walk to the church. He then considered the chores that she would still need to tackle at the end of the day. He suddenly felt guilty for choosing to sleep in instead of going to mass that morning.

"The walk is relaxing," she assured him. "Sometimes I'm able to pray on the way." Like a child sharing a special secret with a friend, she lifted her right hand from her pocket to reveal the white rosary in her grip.

He was not quite sure what to say in response. Getting to know this woman proved to be an edifying experience for him.

She seized upon the moment of silence to announce her intentions. "I have to go."

John wanted to stay and talk with her. He wanted to know how her day was going. He always enjoyed her company. But this was not the time. She had made the long journey to be with the Lord and he would not dare to get in the way.

So in a responsible utilization of his free will, he proceeded to bid her farewell. "See you later Peace. Extend my greetings to Lawrence."

"Bye bye," she answered back.

Within seconds, she disappeared into the church and he suddenly realized that he had forgotten all about his hunger.

CHAPTER 6

Lawrence and I agreed that he would start clearing our fenced parcel on Friday after school. John's help two days ago quickened our progress with the harvests making it possible to start our next project earlier than planned. That Friday afternoon, I passed through our front door on my way to take some water to Lawrence. My thoughts went to John. I could still detect some weariness when I ran into him the previous day and I wondered whether we would ever see him again. To my great surprise, the doctor's jeep arrived in front of our house in a matter of seconds. The plastic cup of water almost fell from my grip as I stood on the porch and watched him exit his vehicle. Clad in a fresh set of work clothes and a smile, he approached me. He stopped just before the first step that led up to the porch.

Good afternoon John," I greeted. As difficult as it was I struggled to keep an even tone. "What brings you here today?" His outfit served as an easy giveaway but I did not want to jump into conclusions.

"I was hoping you would have something for me to do," was his pleasant response. I found it difficult to keep from smiling at the humble way through which he offered his help. Any passerby witnessing our conversation would automatically assume that we were the ones helping him and not vice versa.

"Thank you for wanting to help," I replied.

"Did I get the job?"

I nodded.

"In that case, you're welcome."

With a song in my heart, I strolled to the back of the house and retrieved an extra hoe. I held it towards John. He took the wooden handle. "What's this?" he asked, his gaze examining the metal blade.

"It's a hoe. We are going to plant *gini*."

A knowing smile showed in his face. "You mean black eyed peas."

I nodded. "But first we need to prepare the land. Lawrence has already started, let's go."

We found my brother laboring vigorously while the earth soaked up his sweat. He had already cleared almost half the land and he piled a variety of weeds in a corner of the plot.

After we each passed through the only gate, I went to my brother and held the cup of water over his head, "John is here to help." Lawrence did not say anything. Instead he straightened from his task, and took the cup. He gulped down its contents in a matter of seconds and handed the blue plastic back to me. Only then did he shift his gaze to our visitor. Lawrence did not bother to wipe the beads of sweat that rolled into his eyes. With a straight face he lifted a hand in a salute to John who returned the gesture.

My brother stooped down to resume his task while I explained to John, "We just need to dig up the weeds from their roots. Then we pile them up over there for disposal later." I pointed to the heap in the corner. The doctor's gaze followed my hand. He then watched Lawrence and the ferocity of the boy's movement with amazement. Finally, he moved to the opposite end of the parcel to begin his work. I knew it was time to take my leave.

"I hope you don't mind," I began to John. "I have some work waiting at the house." He gave a shrug which told me that he had no objections to being left alone with my frowning brother.

"Go ahead, don't worry about us," he assured. With some degree of comfort, I turned to leave.

I hurried to the house and dropped the plastic cup in the sink. Then I mounted the narrow stairs to my brother's room. His dirty clothes sat in a heap on the floor next to his bed. I stooped down and directed the pile into my arms. Then with cautious steps, I made my way back to the side of the house where I had already set up three buckets and a stool for my task. With a light thud, the dirty shorts and shirts met the ground. I settled unto the stool that faced the buckets and began my work. My right hand reached for a shirt. I submerged it into the first bucket containing soapy water and began to wash as fast as I could. With John helping at the farm, I knew it would be terribly rude of me to send him home on an empty stomach. Before he arrived, the plan was for me and Lawrence to have some bread and water for dinner. But a few slices of bread would not do anymore. I needed to prepare a meal sufficient for the three of us. I dipped the washed shirt into the second bucket of clear water for rinsing. Then with both hands I wrung the shirt and threw it into the third empty bucket.

Hungry mosquitoes swirled around my face. Quickly, my hand reached for another shirt and flung it about to dissuade the insects. They vanished momentarily only to return to my legs. I was halfway through the load when that piercing sensation invaded my consciousness. This time, I slapped my legs but to no avail. I rose from the stool and paced around for a minute before returning to my task. My thoughts reverted to the men. I left John at the parcel an hour ago. If he worked as fast as Lawrence then they would be back within another hour or two.

A clothes line ran above my head between two metal poles which had been installed by my father. When every garment had passed the rinsing stage, I discarded the used buckets of water. As I hung the clothes to dry, I exhaled in relief that the men had not returned. My brain searched for the quickest meal to prepare but nothing offered itself to my mind. I hung the last pair of shorts and reentered the kitchen. The kitchen cupboard presented a bag of beans, a bag of rice and some corn. My gaze questioned the plastic clock on the wooden counter top. Cooking beans at five thirty in the evening would prove to be a disaster. It would take forty five minutes just to pick out the tiny rocks and wash the beans clean. Boiling the food demanded even more time, usually a few hours. My eyes shifted to the bag of rice. I could cook some rice, but we lacked the catfish for the accompanying stew. Finally my gaze settled on the ears of corn. There were eight of them, each one still concealed in its husk. It would only take a few minutes to roast them. Relief filtered through my being as the plan took shape in my mind. I just needed to start a fire in the backyard.

I grabbed the matchbox and exited through the back door into the small clearing of land known as our backyard. Behind the clearing lay a sea of elephant grass. To this day I do not know where the stretch of toughened grass ends. I stooped before our outdoor cooking spot a few feet from the house. A round iron grill supported by four iron legs stood two feet from the ground. I felt grateful for the leftover firewood that still sat under the grill from our last corn roasting. Within minutes the fire came to life. After several trips to the kitchen, I sat on a bench before the fire with a basin of raw corn beside me and an empty tray for the roasted meal.

The men returned just as the sun was retiring for the day. I could relax a little because four ears of corn mingled with the fire. Lawrence approached first with John lagging behind. When Lawrence arrived, he entered the house. I knew his routine. He could not stand to do anything else after farm work until he had taken a bath. That evening was no different. Eventually, John reached my bench and settled onto the unclaimed portion of the furniture. The look of weariness which possessed his features two days ago, resurfaced. I couldn't help but to feel concern for him. I returned a partially peeled corn back into the basin.

"Would you like some water?"

"Yes please." His words sounded like gasps.

I entered the kitchen and reached for the bottle of previously boiled water on the countertop. Moments later I returned to the backyard with a full plastic cup twice the size of Lawrence's blue cup. I handed it to John who took it with a profound expression of gratitude in his face. Most of the drink entered his stomach, the rest he splashed unto his face.

He handed the plastic back to me. "Thanks a lot. That really helped." As I took the cup from him I observed his smiling face and concluded that he was right. When I returned from the kitchen I used my fork to turn the ears of corn so that the uncooked sections could be roasted.

Then I turned my gaze to John, "I hope you will stay for dinner. Have you ever tried our roasted corn?"

He shook his head. "Nope, but it smells good."

"Anything would smell good after all the work you've done today."

We shared a brief chuckle before he continued, "Your brother works really hard. You should be proud of him." Like a grateful parent indeed, my heart swelled at the words.

"I thank God for Lawrence."

John seemed to turn some thoughts over in his mind. I let him think as I retrieved the roasted corn from the fire and placed them in the tray.

With his gaze fixed on the flames, he spoke, "Can I ask a personal question?" I took great care in setting the rest of the uncooked corn in the fire before answering John.

"You may ask, but I don't guarantee an answer."

His features betrayed some amusement at my response. "Alright....did you always believe the way you do now?"

At first I did not understand. I gave him a puzzled look.

"Your faith," he explained. "Have you always believed in God the way you do now?"

I thought for a while. "I suppose so. When I was a child my mother brought me to God. And He has been my best friend ever since."

In slow nods he took in my answer. Cricket sounds traveled to us from the bushes nearby.

I returned my gaze to the man that sat at the opposite end of the bench. "Why did you ask?"

He shrugged. "Just curious I guess." Soon his curiosity grew infectious for I found myself asking the very same question.

"What about you John, did you always believe?"

With a distant look in his eyes he shook his head.

"What changed your mind?"

"My mother's prayers and her passing"

The questions swirled in my mind. I wanted to know more but I did not posses the courage to pry. My gaze reverted to the corncob in my grip, my fingers absentmindedly pulling away at the husk.

"I know you have questions Peace." How did he learn to understand me so quickly?

I looked up at him, still feeling a little surprised at being found out. "You don't mind?"

He shook his head, "Not at all, I enjoy talking to you."

I turned each ear of corn with my fork, hoping with all my heart that he could not perceive the disconcerting effects of his admission.

When the last had been flipped, I looked at him. "How did your mother's passing change your mind?"

For a moment John lifted his face to look at the stars. Then turning to me he began, "She died five years ago. The day before she died we went shopping at the mall."

I did not know exactly what a mall was but I guessed it was like a market place. I let John go uninterrupted as I listened.

"My priority at the time was to make as much money as possible so that I could retire early and travel the world. I met Sharon at medical school, and we talked of marriage. We were all about the here and now. Neither of us gave much thought to eternity. She was doing well at the women's hospital and I had just joined a practice in an affluent neighborhood. I also kept a part time job at the hospital so money was never an issue for us. My work took up most of my time and I eventually started to feel guilty about neglecting my mother."

A look of sorrow claimed John's face as he spoke. As I listened, I wondered if he was aware of his facial change.

"With my father still teaching at the university, I knew she was lonely in the daytime. On my day off, I finally made the decision to take her to the most expensive clothing store. We spent hours in that store. But she didn't buy a thing. She was more interested in me. We talked the whole time, about life in general, then my life. Every once

63

in a while she would pick up an outfit, examine it and put it back down. By the time we left the store, I realized that the highly expensive stuff did not impress her very much. Regardless, I could see how happy she was that day. From the store we drove to a restaurant for dinner. On our way home I stopped at a gas station and that's when it happened." He paused. The distant look shone in his face.

"What happened?" I asked.

"Someone came to rob the gas station just as we were pulling next to a pump. Neither of us sensed any danger until bullets started flying. The owner of the gas station also had a gun. While he exchanged fire with the robber, a stray bullet passed through the car into my mother's side. In the midst of the gunfire, I did what I could to stop the bleeding. A witness must have called the police. In a short while an ambulance arrived to find a dead robber, a dead business owner and my wounded mother. At the hospital my mother asked me to send for a priest. I did as she wished but I had never been more afraid in my life because we both knew that she was dying. I also called my father. When my dad arrived my mother was in the room talking with the priest. Dad did not go in. She was confessing her sins, neither of us had the right to walk in there.

After the priest left, I stood at the door and watched my parents in their last conversation. She then asked to be alone with me. When I came to her bedside she looked at me with such pleading eyes. I remember asking her what was wrong. But nothing prepared me for what she was about to say." He took a deep breath and exhaled. I sat still, fighting the temptation to prompt him.

After what felt like a decade he began, "She told me how much she loved me and how she had spent years praying for me. She pleaded with me not to waste anymore time and to return to God. She then asked me to rejoice that I did not get hit by a bullet."

John took a break, and shifted his gaze to me. I averted his gaze, unsure of what to say next, or if I should speak at all.

John continued, "You can imagine the shock and confusion I felt at the time. The idea that my soul might be in danger was totally foreign to me. My mother died the next day. But her comments stayed with me for a long time. We came back here to bury her. While we were here I began to confront her words. Why would she fear for my soul? I always considered myself to be a good person. I didn't go around robbing people. I was a nice guy. I told myself these things, but no matter how much money I earned, I never could experience the peace that my parents often possessed.

So in this village I did something that I had not done in years. I began to pray. One day I looked at the crucifix that was mounted on the wall of my uncle's house. For the first time in my life I began to seriously contemplate what it symbolized. Something happened to me during those moments. I don't know how to describe it, but I began to feel sorry for my sins. I went to confession that same day. I was in the confessional for two hours, but when I stepped out I felt so light. A huge burden had been lifted from me and I remember chiding myself for not coming to this great sacrament sooner."

I understood what John meant because I too had experienced numerous blessings from confessing my sins to Jesus in this sacrament.

"Almost instantly," he continued, "my hunger for my Catholic faith increased. I began to read the Scriptures.

I wanted to get as far away as possible from my old life of conceit. During those years I did not realize how or even when I stopped paying attention to God. All I know is that one day I woke up and began to think that I did not need my Creator anymore. You can imagine what I felt when my eyes were reopened to reality. I know now what my mother meant when she asked me to rejoice that night."

Something in his mind caused him to shudder. Then he continued, "It filled me with gratitude to realize that God kept me alive out of His mercy."

"What about Sharon?" I asked, surprising myself.

"Sharon was not very happy when I returned to the US. At first she tried to make things work. She came to church with me a couple of times. But she began to see that this was a lifestyle change and not a phase or some fleeting interest. That's when she left."

"You must have been heartbroken."

John shook his head. "At first it hurt that she wouldn't share in my joy. But there is a kind of peace that comes from obedience to God. Frankly, I wasn't willing to sacrifice that for anyone. Our priorities had become so different. We did the right thing by going our separate ways. Anyway she is married now. I wish her the best, but most of all I pray that she would realize how much God loves her and waits for her."

His gaze was on the fire when he finished. I moved to retrieve the last of our dinner from the flames. In the silent moment that passed I pondered how much of his wounds were reopened by talking about these events that led to his mother's death.

I decided to break the silence by offering some words of comfort. "Thank you for sharing with me John. I am happy for you that you found Jesus. Your mother did not die in vain."

John nodded slowly. "I know she didn't. She is a blessing."

I glanced about me. There was nothing left to do but to call Lawrence. I excused myself and entered the house. Lawrence reclined in the sitting room with a textbook on the coffee table before him and our kerosene lamp by its side.

"Come and eat," I said.

He looked up at me. "Can we eat inside?"

"Of course, I'll just tell John. Please do me a favor and put out the fire." He rose from his seat and followed me through the back door.

I informed John as soon as he came into sight. "We are eating inside. I hope you don't mind."

"Why would I mind?" he smiled. He rose from the bench and carried the furniture into the house. We all pitched in and cleared the backyard. Lawrence brought a bowl of water and some soap for John to wash his hands. Afterwards we gathered at the table for a dinner of corn, bread and mangoes.

An atmosphere of familiarity filled the room as we ate that night. It was as though we were entertaining an old friend and not a guest. Even Lawrence seemed to relax at the table. He ventured to tell a few jokes that kept us tittering throughout dinner. For the first time in three years the walls of our tiny kitchen bore silent witness to the beautiful sound of laughter.

CHAPTER 7

At the time, I did not know why, but I repeatedly told myself that John's concern for us was merely out of compassion. Several weeks passed, and he continued to show up almost on a daily basis to offer his assistance. He remained determined. With time his endurance for manual labor improved. And by the end of the eighth week we sold more produce at the market than Lawrence and I had ever dreamed possible. Even my brother developed a friendship with him. The two would often spend hours chatting about sports or medical science.

One evening as I fried the plantains that would go with our cooked beans, I overheard their conversation in the sitting room.

"Can I ask you something?" started my brother.

"Sure, you can ask me anything," was John's encouraging reply.

My brother cleared his throat. "Achugoa is holding a rally tomorrow at the market."

I froze at the news.

"I know my sister thinks he is bad influence but I'm not fully convinced. Why shouldn't I attend the rally tomorrow?"

My initial thought was to burst into the room and scold Lawrence for even considering going to that meeting, but I received another thought cautioning me to stay put. It took all my will power to continue slicing those plantains.

"Why do you think you should attend?" asked John. His tone was calm, a complete contrast to the effects of adrenalin shooting through my veins.

"Because Achugoa seems to be the only one that is truly concerned about our village, our rulers won't put their feet down. They just look the other way while the Se's continue to settle on our land."

John did not respond immediately to my brother's comments. But when he did, he shared some information that was news even to my own ears.

"It is true that some Ses have expanded their territory near the border. But that stretch of land that you talk of does not belong to our village either. I've driven out there a couple of times to find out what's really going on. I have also visited the city to study the maps. From what I understand the area in question belonged to neither village until a few Ses decided to farm it. Going over there to attack them would only hurt more people. In that village there are people like you and your sister. They do not want any trouble. They don't even support what a handful of their citizens are doing at the border. If Achugoa's plan was to become a reality, those peaceful people are the ones that would most likely suffer. They are the ones that would lose their loved ones, their wives, sisters, brothers, children, or even their parents."

John stopped at the mention of parents. In the silence I hoped his point would penetrate Lawrence's mind. I wanted my brother to put himself in the place of our so called enemies. They too had lost their loved ones and their properties in the previous conflict. The majority of them did not want another war.

A few minutes passed without a word from my brother. Did he recognize the truth in John's statements?

Then with a troubled sigh Lawrence broke the silence, "Achugoa says that if we ignore them they will continue to expand until they cross into our village and take over our land."

"He doesn't know that to be a fact," replied John, "I think our chiefs should open up a dialogue with their rulers so that an agreement can be reached. My uncle and aunt have been working hard to get that message across to our leaders. They need our prayers and our fasts. No one needs to take up arms in order for this problem to be resolved."

As John continued to speak with my brother in his calm tone, I felt my heart resume its normal pace. The conversation would have taken on a different form if John had been absent. Lawrence and I would have exchanged words with neither of us listening to the other and he would eventually become frustrated and storm out of the house to meet the very people that wanted another bloodbath. But he was not going anywhere that night. Instead he remained seated and allowed himself to listen to John.

I sliced the last of the plantains and placed them in a frying pan of heated oil. A crackling sound erupted, interrupting the flow of their conversation to my ears.

The men were still talking when I stepped into the sitting room moments later.

"The food is ready," I announced. Lawrence rose first, followed by John. I moved the lamp from the countertop to the center of the kitchen table where we all gathered. John led Grace.

Minutes passed and the only sound in the room came from our spoons as they clashed against our plates. My brother sat at one end of the table and ate with his face down. I studied him. His silent withdrawal told me that he experienced some sort of conflict. Perhaps he wrestled John's argument against Achugoa's. I kept my eyes on him, hoping for any words concerning the thoughts that busied his mind. As I watched my brother, I wasn't aware that John also observed me until I looked in the opposite end of the table where he sat. I recognized that look of concern that he had so often lavished upon me. He offered a comforting smile which melted my heart.

Then he went on to break the silence, "Peace, your cooking is really good." Turning to my brother he added, "Right Lawrence?" The boy raised his face toward John. He delivered an unenthusiastic nod before lifting a spoon of seasoned beans to his mouth.

But John was not giving up so easily. "Hey Lawrence," he began in a casual tone. "Remember that soccer team we talked about, the red lions?"

The boy offered another stoic nod.

"They are playing tomorrow. My uncle cancelled on me so I'm left with an extra ticket which would go to waste unless you decide to come along."

The offer did nothing to improve my brother's mood. With a frown he answered,

"Tomorrow is Friday, a school day."

"The game starts at four o'clock, replied John. "If I pick you up after school, you'll have more than enough time to come home and change before we head off to central stadium."

At the mention of the venue, I turned to the boy, "Central stadium! Oh Lawrence you've always wanted to visit central stadium!"

A look of uncertainty settled in my brother's face as he weighed the offer. He shifted his gaze to me.

"What about the farm?" he asked.

I smiled to reassure Lawrence. I knew exactly what he was doing. Whenever he was faced with the idea of doing something that he wasn't too keen on, he would find excuses to discourage himself from the prospect. Despite my smile, I felt shaken at the reality of Achugoa's stronghold on my brother. It was out of character for my brother to hesitate in matters involving soccer. If this offer had been made to Lawrence a year ago, he would have accepted it without a second thought. I never thought I would see the day when he would think twice at the idea of attending a soccer event.

I wasted no time in encouraging him to attend. "I can manage for one day. Besides I may not be here for dinner. By the grace of God, I plan on going over to the neighbor's in the evening. Charity wants me to braid her hair tomorrow."

Lawrence dropped his gaze to his plate. For what seemed like an eternity I sat still, holding my breath and awaiting his decision.

John and I exchanged glances. He shared my suspense. "So, what do you think?" he asked to Lawrence.

At this question, my brother lifted his face devoid of any humor, and answered, "I don't want that ticket to be wasted."

I closed my eyes and released a huge sigh of relief.

CHAPTER 8

The next day John picked Lawrence up from school and they stopped by our house for a brief moment before driving off to the city.

Later that evening I walked for ten minutes to Charity's house and absentmindedly braided her hair. My heart rejoiced that Lawrence would not be present at the rally to hear Achugoa's troublesome speeches. Perhaps this was the beginning of the end, the end of Lawrence's involvement with the troublemakers.

On Monday morning, as I washed the breakfast dishes, the sound of someone knocking on the door traveled to my ears. *Who could be calling at nine thirty in the morning?* I quickly dried my hands on my apron and went to find out. To my surprise John stood at the other side of the door. *What is he doing here so early? He never came by until after Lawrence returned from school.* His countenance was serious yet troubled as we exchanged morning greetings.

"Good morning, Peace. I hope you don't mind that I came by."

"No, of course not, you are always welcome in our home. But there is no one home besides me."

With my brother absent, I decided that staying on the front porch was the best idea. There seemed to be an unspoken understanding between us for he too did not try to enter the house. I thankfully stepped onto the porch.

"Something is wrong." I said. From the look in his eyes I could tell that whatever he was about to say would bring forth tears.

"I have to return to the US at once." I felt like something had just knocked the wind out from me.

"But why? This is so sudden."

"My dad has just suffered a heart attack, and things don't look good."

"Oh dear," my eyes watered at the news. As I looked at John, I could only imagine his pain at receiving such news and not being able to be by his father's side at that very moment.

"I'm very sorry."

John took a deep breath and exhaled. "Don't cry," he asked softly. "I've been praying for him since the news came before dawn this morning."

Feeling annoyed with myself I dried my tears with the tips of my fingers. I should be the one comforting him and not vice versa. I proceeded to offer the same advice that sustained me in my times of difficulty. "Don't stop praying. Put everything in God's hands."

He nodded.

Then I mustered up the courage to ask, "When do you leave?"

"First thing tomorrow morning, but I have something to ask you."

"What is it John?" He brought his gaze to my eyes. I recognized that look of care in its most earnest form.

"I know we've only known each other a few months. I've prayed about this day and night and I am convinced without a doubt that you are the one for me. So I come here today, hoping that you feel the same way, to ask you to marry me."

He paused, but all I could do was gape. "I am in love with you," he continued, the affection dominating his voice. "All through my life I have never met a woman as considerate, as courageous, and as kind as you are Peace. I have watched you care for others. I have watched you work tirelessly to keep your home and your land. You understand that you are a child of God and believe me it is reflected in the humility and dignity through which you conduct yourself. You are so beautiful, and yet you are much more beautiful on the inside."

When he paused again, his eyes filled with moisture. "You thank me for helping out on the farm. But it has been my pleasure to enjoy your hospitality, to spend time with you. I am the grateful one. I would be very honored if you allowed me the privilege of taking care of you and your brother. I recognize how important he is to you, and I would never cause the two of you to be separated."

At these words my tears returned.

"What do you say?" he asked. "Will you be my wife? I would be so honored if you agreed to become Mrs. John Williams."

As I gazed up at him, I finally admitted to myself that I did love him. I fought it day and night out of fear of what would become of Lawrence if I married. The subject was too painful to contemplate, so I had resorted to denial.

But looking into his eyes, thinking of the comfortable way in which we laughed, prayed and worked together, I knew how very much I loved this man standing before me. Throughout his time with us, he never once gave us a reason to doubt his integrity. John really gave of himself to us, taking on tasks which were especially grueling for him. He didn't have to roll up his sleeves and plough our parcel with us. He never once complained about the intense labor or its duration.

Day after day he came back to help us and as each week passed I saw the calluses appear on his hands. During the harvests, I once observed him grimace in pain and rub his shoulders, but that never stopped him. He had become one of us, even making Lawrence's wellbeing a concern of his. I felt that he had come to understand me in a special way. Sometimes we would exchange glances, and he would know, without my saying a word, when something threatened to trouble my mind. I never felt the need to be someone else in his presence. But most of all we shared the most important goal. What could be more attractive in a man than his sincere desire to be faithful to Jesus and to His church?

"Yes!" I answered, "I will marry you." Emotion brought a great deal of hoarseness to my throat causing my words to come out like a whisper. I nodded vigorously to emphasize my answer.

Like the rising sun following a bout of heavy rain, the joy came in and settled in his face. With the back of his hand he wiped the tears that threatened to roll down his cheek.

"You have no idea how fortunate you've made me."

On that porch John and I laughed, cried and laughed again. At length we sat side by side on the bench.

We didn't care that a lizard had just lost its balance from the roof and landed, on its feet, right onto our porch floor. The orange-headed creature performed its usual nods before crawling off into oblivion.

John took my hand. "My uncle should know before hand if things become unstable around here. I made arrangements with them to get you and Lawrence to safety before any fighting breaks out. They own a home in the city, and they're happy to accommodate you and Lawrence until I can return to meet you both." With a gentle squeeze of my hand he continued, "If things don't get worse, I will return as soon as possible so that we can start marriage preparations. What do you think?"

He had my admiration right then for thinking of our safety ahead of time. "You've really thought this through haven't you?"

With that contemplative gaze he answered, "Everyday for the past month"

"Oh John, I'm grateful for your thoughtfulness but I hope we would never have to leave."

"I hope so too. I meant what I said earlier about settling here and starting a clinic. When I got on the plane to come here, my intentions were to finalize things. I came back to buy some land."

I looked up at him. "Did you?"

He nodded. Then with some regret in his voice he continued, "I wish I could have shown it to you."

"Don't worry. I will see the land if and when God wants me to."

He looked at me with a smile. "I am in love with a wise woman."

"And I'm in love with a kind, handsome man."

We ate roasted corn on the porch and eagerly awaited my brother's return. The sun started its decent, but the boy was still nowhere to be seen. Eventually John had to leave to prepare for his journey. With tears streaming down my cheeks I followed him to the jeep. It pained me to see him leave, but I understood.

"I will be praying for your father and for you," I assured.

John tenderly brushed the tears from my cheeks. "My dear Peace, I know."

With a heavy heart I watched him drive off without knowing exactly the date of his intended return. As soon as I reentered the house my knees met the floor and I clasped both hands together in prayer.

"Father in Heaven, Healer of all, please hear our prayers for John's earthly father. He is ill, Lord, and needs Your healing touch. Please heal his body and soul. Dearest God I know that nobody loves him more than You do. I know that You want the best for him. So with confidence I entrust him into Your hands Dear Lord and I pray that Your Will for him will be fulfilled. Please take John safely to his side. Amen."

My brother finally returned that night with an explanation. He talked of some extra school work that he needed to complete at the library. I wasted no time in sharing the news with him. He seemed happy. But when I entered his bedroom later that night to gather up his dirty laundry, I caught him sitting upright with an intense gaze fixed on the wall and his hands clasped under his chin.

"What's wrong?" I'd asked.

My brother pretended to smile. "Nothing"

I found it hard to believe him, but he insisted that all was fine.

During the next week Lawrence continued to return home at later hours.

"You know how it is towards the end of term," he often said. "People study into the night." An unsettling feeling troubled me. What if he was not studying like he said? And if he wasn't studying what was he doing? The possible answer turned my stomach. Several times I took the long way home from the market in order to pass the library and each time his bicycle stood outside the meager building with that of the other students. Maybe I was overreacting. After all I graduated from the same secondary school. Things did get competitive during the final exams.

Since we had no phone in our home, any communication between John and I passed through his aunt. His father survived the heart attack, but remained in a doctor's care. John was doing his best to be a son and not a doctor.

"He misses you so much," reported Mrs. Ebem. "If only you could hear him for yourself." I missed him too and I looked forward to his return, little did I know what lay ahead.

CHAPTER 9

One morning, the Ebem's driver arrived at our house. I had just finished checking on the goats and was making my way back to the house when I saw the slender man approaching. He could not have been much older than John but the grief from losing most of his family in the previous conflict, carved out premature wrinkles and fine lines in his face.

"I'm over here," I called from the side of the house.

He stopped in his tracks toward the front door and nodded to me in greeting.

"Good morning Adam," I replied as my steps brought me to where he stood.

He did not wait for me to ask why he was visiting that morning.

"Boss say make I bring you for house."

That nauseating feeling invaded my stomach at once. It was terribly unusual for the Ebem's to just send for me out of the blues.

"What's wrong," I asked. "Did something happen?"

The man shrugged his shoulders and continued in Pidgin English. "Sista, I no fit tell you." He shook his head vehemently. "I suppose bring you for house now, now!"

I studied the man. The look of determination in his face revealed the futility of my asking any more questions.

"Okay," I answered, hurrying toward our front door. "Let me get my bag."

I reached the Ebem's brown stucco house to find them already waiting for me in their living room. Their faces bore grim expressions. Mrs. Ebem sat next to her husband, her right hand fanning vigorously.

"Be seated," said the man. I sank into a leather chair adjacent to their couch. He went straight to the point. "The chiefs are going to declare war on the Se people."

Those words drained the energy from my muscles. "Why would they do such a thing after what we've all suffered just three years ago?"

The man shook his head with pity. "We tried to reason with them. Their decision is a complete mystery to me." I glanced at his wife who continued to fan herself in silence.

"We are leaving," he stated. "You and Lawrence are coming with us. There is no time to waste." It hurt terribly to have to leave the only place I knew to be home, but it was clear that there was no other option."

I stirred up the courage. "What do we do?"

"Go home and pack all your things tonight. We will pick you and Lawrence up tomorrow morning on our way into the city.

Be sure to inform as many people as possible. Tell them to get out while they can."

Adam was kind enough to drop me off at the neighbor's so that I could warn them. Upon entering the house, I found my friend Charity weeping in the living room. She held out her hands to me and let out very agonizing screams. I put my arms around her shoulders to comfort her. Several times I asked what the source of her pain was, but she could not bring herself to speak.

It took a good hour for her to calm down. I then entered her kitchen and fixed her a cup of tea. After the first sip of the drink she raised those swollen eyes to me.

"My husband has gone to fight. I pleaded with him on my knees, but he would not listen. He said that he was doing the right thing. He said he was doing what any man in our village should do...." Her voice trailed off. I remained speechless while she lifted the tremulous cup to her mouth. At length she looked at me.

"He asked me to travel south and wait for him."

I spent the next hour comforting the young wife before visiting the other neighbors to warn them.

I arrived home to find Lawrence in his room packing his things. He already knew about the chiefs' decision. I retreated to my own room to do likewise. Inside my bedroom, my eyes caught sight of the framed picture of mama and me that I kept on the side table. I picked it up and ran my fingers across mama's youthful face. I must have been four years old at the time. My mind recalled that day like it was yesterday. We had attended a wedding and one of the guests went around taking pictures of everyone. He came to our parents as they stood chatting with other adults. I wanted to be part of the fun but all I could see were shoes. With determination I pulled on mama's maternity dress. My mother looked down at me. "What is it dear?"

With outstretched arms I made known my request, "Carry me."

I remember her swaying her head. "I can't."

Despite her gentle tone, my eyes watered at the answer. "Why?"

With a thoughtful look on her face she took my hand and excused herself from the conversation. She led me to a nearby aluminum chair and sat down.

Placing a hand on her bulging tummy she explained, "There is a baby in there. That means I cannot carry many things because it could disturb the baby and he could get hurt. You are going to be a big sister."

With a heightened curiosity I stared at her tummy. "Why is he hiding in there?"

Mama's dimples appeared as she chuckled. "He is not hiding. He will come out when the time is right. You too used to live in my tummy."

I stared at her. This was news to me. I marveled at the revelation that there was once a time when mama's tummy was my home.

She wrapped her arms around me. "The baby's life is very precious just like yours and mine. Will you help me keep him safe?" With eagerness I nodded. Mother placed a kiss on my forehead. And at that moment the photographer took the picture of us.

Tears filled my eyes. Those were happy times, a stark contrast to the days that lay ahead. If only we could just live in peace. If only we could just keep our eyes on Jesus and obey His commandments. Why couldn't we just respect the lives that God has so lovingly created? And as for me, what part did I play in all of this? Did I spend too much time talking about this conflict and not enough time praying and fasting for its aversion? Still clutching mama's picture, I allowed my exhausted body to slump into my bed. My heart wept for all the families that were warned today. They would all flee their homes and occupations to go and face tougher hardship elsewhere. I buried my face in my pillow and sobbed like never before.

The following morning, I ladled porridge into two bowls. An atmosphere of sorrow filled the room but I constantly reminded myself to be grateful, we had a comfortable place to flee to. I strode to the bottom of the stairs and called out to my brother.

"Come down for breakfast!" There was no answer.

I called out again. "Hurry down. The Ebems should be here any minute!" He still gave no answer. I then mounted the stairs toward his bedroom. He still did not respond to my raps on the door. *Maybe he has overslept.* I pushed the door open to find nothing in the room. With my heart racing I approached his closet. It was empty. His suitcase was gone. I dashed to the bathroom and back to his room. There were no signs of my brother. His room looked like it had never been inhabited.

Oh no," I cried. Wondering what to do, I clasped my trembling hands together and glanced around. My eyes caught sight of a piece of paper on the mattress.

I dashed to it and snatched it up. "This is Lawrence's writing!" With trembling hands I read the words.

Peace,

> *By the time you find this note I will be miles away. I have gone to do what I've always intended. And that is to fight for our village. Please do not attempt to find me. Proceed with your plans to leave with the Ebem's. You have been a good mother, sister, and friend to me. John is a nice man and I wish you both the best. Perhaps we*

shall meet again after the battle has been won. We do not intend to lose. Understand that I have to do this. What happened to mama and papa should never have happened to anybody. That is why I am fighting, to ensure it never repeats again.

-till we meet again
Lawrence

The note fell from my hands and I lost consciousness. When my eyes finally opened, I was lying in bed with Mrs. Ebem by my bedside.

"How are you feeling?" she asked. I tried to speak but my throat felt like sandpaper. She seemed to perceive my troubles and brought me a cup of water.

"You fainted," she offered.

Then it all came back to me, Lawrence left to have him self killed!

"He's gone!" I began screaming inconsolably.

The woman wrapped her arms around me. "It's okay," she whispered. "We found the note. My husband is out looking for him, rest." But how could I rest under the circumstances? I broke away from her embrace and tried to leave the bed, but dizziness overwhelmed me. My hand grabbed the bed to keep from falling.

"You see what I mean?" said the woman as she coaxed me back into bed. "You need food and rest." She pulled the covers to my chin and left the room. Minutes later she returned with some porridge. I ate, not out of hunger, but out of the desire to join the search for my brother. An hour later I was on my feet and out of the house. I visited the home of Lawrence's classmates. They, too, had disappeared. At midday, I returned home in tears and waited. Mr. Ebem's Mercedes pulled up three hours later. The tightness in his face told it all.

As he approached us he shook his head. "Your brother does not want to be found. I searched the known training camps run by Achugoa. The boy asked to be transferred to an undisclosed location this morning." He scratched his beard. "It's a pity." His voice carried a tone of finality, a tone which I was not ready to accept. The man looked at me, and I knew his thoughts.

I began to shake my head vehemently. "No. I will not leave my brother. That is just impossible."

"Please you have to come with us," begged his wife.

I continued shaking my head. "You do not understand, he may return, and I want to be here when he comes. I cannot leave him alone." For hours I continued to talk in this fashion.

I begged the Ebems to leave without me. But they pleaded and persuaded until it became clear that I was dead serious. Before they departed Mrs. Ebem wailed as though she would never see me alive again. I cried too, especially for all the pain my decision would bring to John.

CHAPTER 10

Two days later our men began fighting up north at the border near the Se village. The Se fighters were prepared and they fought back with ferocity. From the village announcer, we received reports of the deaths on both sides. The news broke my heart. I spent my time praying for the souls that were departing from the earth.

I was surprised to find that Charity did not head south as her husband had instructed. Everyday the two of us would wait anxiously for news of our loved ones. Our homes stood at the south end of the village near the border to the neighboring country. As a result our lives remained relatively quiet except for the daily arrival of the black beat-up lorry which carried casualties to their heart broken families. We spent most of our time sharing our food with others. One night I sat alone in the kitchen with all the money made from past sales strewn before me. It was all useless now. The market had once again been reduced to a huge pile of rubble. Most farmers had fled, and there was nowhere else to buy food.

Just as I feared, the casualties increased by staggering numbers causing more villagers to head south to the neighboring country. Word spread that a refugee camp had been set up there. One evening as Charity and I sat down to eat our dinner of peanuts and water, the dreaded black lorry pulled up before my home. With a pounding heart I ran through the front door and unto the porch, but my feet would not move any further. The driver, a grey haired man nodded to me in greeting. I recognized our parish priest on the passenger seat. The men disembarked and approached us.

The priest's face was somber. "I'm very sorry," he began. My knees gave way at once. I fell to ground and wailed. Charity knelt beside me. My cries drowned out her words of comfort. The men returned to the truck and retrieved my brother's corpse on a stretcher. I could barely recognize him. Shaggy hair concealed his face and a bloodstained bandage circled around his gaunt waist. They placed him before me on the ground and I wrapped my arms around him.

As I knelt in the dirt with Lawrence's body in my arms, our whole life together flashed before me. I saw him again as the bubbly infant whom I could not wait to get home from school to play with. I saw the adventurous seven year old boy who showed me how to catch grasshoppers in our yard without harming them. He would cradle the insects in his palms, taking care not to hurt them before they were released again. We perfected our cartwheels and back flips together, grew up together, joked together, and worked together until Achugoa and his followers came along.

"We have to stop this!" I cried. We must stop killing each other!" My screams attracted a small crowd. I continued to wail until my throat became sore.

The driver returned to the truck and sat with growing impatience. "We have other stops," he said to the priest.

The priest took a glance at us and back at the driver. "Give me a few more minutes to speak with her." He returned to where I knelt with Lawrence in my arms. Tears still dripped down my face.

"Your brother experienced deep contrition before he died. He confessed his sins," offered the priest in a compassionate tone. I nodded in gratitude, but could not think clearly to answer him.

He reached in his pocket and pulled out a note. "Lawrence dictated this for you just before he died." I snatched it from his hand. The priest said something about a burial, but all I could think about was the content of the note. Once he left I quickly unfolded it. My senses fell numb to its surroundings. I did not even hear the lorry's struggling engine as it rolled away leaving a trail of black smoke.

My dear sister,

> *I am very sorry. Please forgive me for causing you so much trouble. You*

were right.   Violence is not the answer! So many people have died. I am so sorry.

Love,
Lawrence

I clutched the note in my palm and wept. Later that evening the priest returned for a funeral that only Charity and I attended. Lawrence was laid to rest in the village graveyard. As the three of us left the burial site the priest warned us to leave the area.

"It's no longer safe here," he said. The Se soldiers are closing in and destroying whatever they find.

"What about you?" I asked. "Aren't you going to leave?"

He shook his head. "This is where I am needed."

"But what if you die?" asked Charity.

He only shrugged. "Then I die." We thanked the kind man for all his help before he parted ways with us.

That night I suffered the temptations of despair. *"You have no parents, no brother, no John, nobody"* said a nasty voice in my mind. *"What is the need to carry on? Why must you flee now? Stay here and await your death. Nobody would care if you lived or died. Charity is around now, but once her husband returns she will desert you in a heartbeat. It's your entire fault anyways, you allowed Lawrence to get mixed up with the wrong crowd. You should have been watching him like a good parent would. It's your entire fault!"*

I crouched down on the cold cement floor, the tears falling from my face. "Please, save me Lord." Just then I thought of my Lord Jesus covered with blood and carrying His heavy cross up Calvary. I knew at once that I too must carry on. Jesus did not give up in the face of sufferings much more severe than mine would ever be; sufferings which He endured for my sake and for the sake of others. And even then He did not stop there. He has loved me unceasingly since before I was born. Countless times I saw several manifestations of His Love in my life. No, I would not despair; to do so would be disastrous.

I felt a sudden strengthening within me. I wiped my eyes and I rose to my feet. Without warning, Charity barged into the living room accompanied by her husband. They carried a small sack.

"You forgot to lock the door," she gasped. I stared at Marcus and wondered whether his presence meant the end of the war.

The terror in his eyes contradicted my thoughts. "We must leave now," he warned. "They're going from house to house in this direction taking prisoners. Quick! Gather what you can, we don't have time!" I raced upstairs and slipped on my canvas shoes. I was about to pack some extra clothing when the sound of gunfire reached my ears. Marcus ran up the stairs and pounded against my door.

"Come now!" he yelled. "They are next door!" Within seconds we dashed down the stairs, out the back door, through the backyard, and into the bush. The three of us raced through the sea of elephant grass like antelopes chased by hungry lions. With the moon as our only source of light, we raced on ignoring the pain caused by the grass as it sliced against our skins. There was no time to think. We just ran to stay alive. Neither of us stopped till about a mile later when we emerged from the field of grass deeper into the forest. Trees! An endless stretch of trees were all my eyes could identify under the moonlight.

We struggled to catch our breaths. Fear gripped me. Even though I had stopped running my heart rate remained accelerated. I never imagined that I would one day find myself in the middle of the forest. What kind of animals dwelt here? Were they poisonous? What if the fighters had followed us? My eyes darted in all directions. Something crawled on the back of my neck. My adrenalin raced. I let out a panicked scream as my hand reached behind my neck and brushed vigorously. There was nothing there. It was all my imagination.

Marcus clasped his toughened hand over my mouth. "What's wrong with you?" he hissed. "Are you trying to get us all killed?" I shook my head. He let go of my mouth.

Still trembling from the experience I mustered up the courage to whisper, "I'm sorry. I thought I felt something crawling on my neck." Charity placed her hand on my shoulder. She seemed much calmer than her husband.

Perspiration dripped down my face. I imagined my companions were also drenched in sweat. The stinging pain set in, salty perspiration mixed with fresh skin cuts. But it was nothing compared to the pain of losing Lawrence. I felt as though my heart would explode from within me. I wanted so much to rest my legs. We stopped our panting and listened carefully for any sign of the fighters. The only sounds that traveled to us came from the crickets and the toads.

"It is better to pray than to despair." Those words came to mind. I clasped my trembling hands together. God is everywhere. He knows everything. He knows our plight. I prayed silently, reminding myself to trust Jesus. I prayed the Lord's Prayer. Then I began to recite the Twenty Third Psalm. As I prayed, my heart felt encouraged. The fear that threatened to paralyze me a moment ago subsided and hope settled in its place. I needed to believe now more than ever. In order to remain calm I needed to believe everything that I understood to be true. God is bigger than anything. He made the whole world, the sun, the moon and the whole universe. He parted the red sea. He made water come forth from a rock. He died for me on the cross. And on the third day He rose from the dead. He loves me. His Love never changes. And even if my flesh was to perish in this place it would not be the end. Because His Grace enabled me to keep returning to Him, each time I fell, through the Sacrament of Reconciliation.

I whispered to the married couple, "What do we do now?"

Marcus pulled out his rusty compass and peered into it. "We have to keep going," he answered.

"We are in the middle of nowhere. Use the flashlight." suggested his wife who was still breathless.

"Do you want to be detected?" he asked." Neither of us dared to argue with him.

At length he lifted his gaze from the compass. "We should go this way." He pointed in a direction but it was too dark to tell which way he meant. Charity took my arm. We huddled close together and walked behind Marcus. He seemed to know what he was doing so neither of us bothered to question him. I only prayed that God would guide him.

Several times I felt crawly things on my skin, but I did not scream anymore. I still jumped occasionally before brushing my hands over my skin. Mosquitoes swarmed around my ears. We stumbled through branches, rocks, or logs, our hands slapping away at the unrelenting insects till daybreak. I clapped for joy when I saw the rays of sunlight sneaking through the branches. *Glory be to God in the highest! We made it through the night!*

We journeyed on through the bush mostly after dark to avoid being caught. In the daytime we hid from bullets and in the nighttime we remained cautiously aware of stinging animals. By the third day my textile dress had become so dirty that its original color of blue was no more. We grew too tired to speak to each other. Charity had to be carried by her husband for her exhaustion was complete. Our loaf of bread was gone, my head pounded like thunder and my skin itched mercilessly from insect bites. Through the Grace of God we trudged on until the sound of people nearby became audible. It was not like the dreaded sound of the fighters or their gunfire. I could hear children playing and mothers chattering to one another. Marcus guessed it must be the village of Carlma in the neighboring country.

We stepped out of the bushes to behold a dirt compound with a main house and three smaller cement houses scattered around it. I knew at once that Charity's husband was right for this was how the Carlma people lived; the parents in the main house, then the married sons each with their respective families in the smaller houses. Three women relaxed under a tree in conversation. We approached them with caution for we had no idea how they would react. The one facing our direction froze with a dropped jaw causing the others to turn around. All three women gaped at us. It was only then that I became aware of the scratch marks on my arms and legs caused by the elephant grass. We stared back, our eyes pleading. Finally, the one who saw us first rose and helped to carry Charity into the main house. I breathed a sigh of relief and thanked God in my heart.

CHAPTER 11

Inside the main house we passed through an open room which except for a few woven mats on the concrete floor lacked furnishings. Our kind host led us down the dark hallway to a small bedroom. After spending three days in the woods, I almost leapt for joy at the sight of the twin mattresses on the floor. Marcus stooped to place his wife in one of the covered foams.

As soon as Charity's flesh touched the sheets our host began to speak. Only then did I notice that we shared the same complexion. Her graying hair was corn rolled into a bun and she donned a purple and white tie-die dress that extended down to her ankles.

The woman placed a hand on her collar bone. "I am the mama of this household." We understood that she was the oldest female in this family.

Pointing a finger to Charity, the woman asked, "What happened to her?" Mama looked to Marcus for an answer. To my surprise he looked to me. Marcus shifted uncomfortably; he did not have the desire to speak.

His kept his gaze on the floor while I tried my best to summarize our experience within the past few days. As I explained, the woman's eyes widened in shock, and almost instantly a profound look of sympathy settled in her face.

"Poor children!   You mean you have been in the bush for three days!"

I nodded.

"It is a miracle that you came out unharmed!" She shuddered at her own words, while I praised God in my heart.

Glory be to the Father and to the Son and to the Holy Spirit, as it was in the beginning is now and ever shall be world without end! Amen!

The two younger women joined us in the room. One of them carried a hot bowl of pepper soup while the other held a towel and a bowl of water.

"These are my son's wives," explained mama.   She pointed to the soup carrying woman, "Her name is Mimi, she is married to my oldest son," and motioning to the unusually large window she continued, "Those are her daughters playing outside."

Mama shifted her gaze to the second woman and explained, "This is my middle son's wife. She has been with us for only a month. We call her Smallwife and she will retain that title until my third son marries." Smallwife smiled shyly at us. She moved to place the bucket next to the mattress where Charity lay.   Even though my friend was visibly conscious, she remained silent throughout the introductions. Mama took the soup bowl from Mimi. She strategically positioned herself on the mattress next to Charity. We all held our breaths and watched Charity accept the first spoon. I exhaled in relief that she had not lost her appetite and still had the strength to take nourishment.

Mama said something to Smallwife in a language that I could not understand. Almost instantly Smallwife came to me and placed her hand on my shoulder.

"Come," she said in a voice as timid as her smile. "I will give you a dress." I took one last glance at Charity before leaving the room. In silence I followed Smallwife out of the house.

In a few hours all three of us were bathed and dressed in clean clothes provided by our hosts. We met the women and their children at the main house for a dinner consisting of roasted yams and tomato stew. They explained to us that the men left just a few minutes before we arrived to hunt for fish. They would not return for the night. Charity and I shared the bedroom in one of the smaller houses while Marcus slept on a mat in its living room.

To my surprise I could not bring myself to fall asleep that night. My thoughts went to Lawrence and then to the people who may have been captured by the Ses. My thoughts also remained with those who did not make it out alive, those little ones of our village, those who escaped like we did but are probably still yet to find a place of refuge. With all these things in my mind I lay on my mattress in the dark quiet room and prayed for many hours.

Sleep eventually came but it was the brief kind. Half way through my slumber I felt a hand nudging my shoulder. I jolted into a sitting position. For a second my mind tricked me into thinking that we were still in the woods, running for our lives. Then I heard Charity's voice coming from the mattress next to mine.

"Are you alright?" It surprised me that she would even be awake in the middle of the night.

"Yes," I answered. "How about you, how come you are not sleeping?"

"You sounded like you were crying." Her ruffled voice limned concern.

My hand brushed the sweat from my face. "Sorry, I did not mean to wake you," I said, a little surprised at myself.

Charity was not upset at being disturbed. "Its okay," she answered. Silent minutes passed. We each knew that the other was awake but neither of us cared for a conversation until Charity asked the question.

"Who is John?"

"Why did you ask that?"

"You talked in your sleep, you said; I am sorry John."

I covered my face with the cotton cloth on loan from Smallwife. Answering Charity's question proved to be too difficult. I felt emotions welling up inside me and it was all I could do to keep from bursting into tears.

"John is the foreigner isn't he?" Without waiting for an answer she continued, "I saw him call on you many times. He acted like a suitor with all those visits, except that we did not see him bring the usual gifts." When I still did not answer Charity continued, "He didn't bring any goats or chickens right?"

"No," I answered, still fighting to hide my sobbing.

"We thought he would, Marcus and I. But he left so suddenly. I waited for you to tell me the news but when you didn't say anything to me I assumed that there was nothing to be said, until now." She paused. I remained still, awaiting the one question that plagued my friend's curiosity.

"Did he state his intentions?"

"Yes," my answer came in a whisper.

"What did he say? Did he ask you to marry him?"

Her questions made audible my silent sobs which I had been trying so hard to keep from my new roommate.

In an agitated voice she concluded, "He asked you to marry him! I should have known. Oh why didn't you tell me? Why have you chosen to suffer alone?" I knew that I did not suffer alone because Christ has always been close to me and He would never leave me in this passing time of my life.

Poor John, oh how much pain I must have caused him! With my face pressed against the pillow I wept freely, my tears soaking up the fabric in an accelerated pace. I did not notice Charity leave her mattress to sit next to my lying form. She placed a hand on my shoulder. And in a sympathy filled voice she asked, "You loved him didn't you?"

My head moved to a nod.

"Did he love you?" she asked next. Again I jounced my head. She seemed at a loss for words. When I calmed down a few minutes later, I heard her weeping too. She stayed up with me and we prayed for John.

"He will be fine," she comforted, after we completed our supplication to the Lord.

My heart agreed with her words. That night I experienced gratitude for such a friend.

We talked further into the night until Charity's eyes could no longer stay open. Eventually she returned to her mattress and drifted off to sleep. Sleep did not come as easily for me that night. I remained awake for a while longer, my mind still processing our experiences over the past few days. The ordeal was terrifying at first. But the experience left me believing even more in the divine mercy of Jesus. He is the only reason why I did not despair after Lawrence's funeral. He is the only reason why I did not lose my mind amidst the darkness that seemed to envelope us in the bush. He is the only reason why I did not lose hope when faced with an endless stretch of trees and it seemed like we would never get out. He is the only reason why we made it out alive. It was not a coincidence that we emerged from the bush into the residence of a family willing to help us. We could have emerged into a deserted road, or even worse into the hands of unwelcoming people. But that did not happen. Not only did Jesus bring about Lawrence's contrition, but the Lord also made it possible for me to learn about it. I will forever be grateful to Jesus. I must try my best to be faithful to Him. I must try my best to resist whatever temptation that may come my way from the enemy, the flesh or the world. Even as I made the resolutions I asked Jesus to help me to keep them. Only His grace could make it possible. Because of the Divine Mercy of Jesus Christ, I have the volition to hope!

CHAPTER 12

At eleven thirty on a Monday night John's plane touched the soil of the nation responsible for educating and shaping his departed mother. He had never felt more grateful to arrive safely at his destination. After enduring thirteen hours in the clouds, John could hardly wait to begin his search for the woman whose plight had him rushing back months ahead of his scheduled arrival.

He recalled that harrowing phone conversation with his aunt, the one that sent him packing. When he heard his aunt Florence's voice, he expected to learn from her that everyone was fine. However, her tone convinced him otherwise and instead he heard the most dreaded words of his life. "The chiefs opted for war." Almost instantly he started to think of ways to help his people. But aunt Florence had one more thing to say, "Peace refused to come with us." The second statement froze him.

The effect of the news felt like a major blow in his stomach. As he listened to his aunt tell the whole story he knew without question that he would have to start travel arrangements as soon as possible. For days, his patience endured trials until his travel agent finally informed him that the earliest flight would depart from New York in three weeks time. Flying out from the empire state presented an inconvenience considering that he had his condo in Atlanta. But the extra step in his itinerary seemed like nothing compared to his reason for wanting to travel.

There were times during his flight when he thought he would succumb to anxiety, but then he would remember Peace's faith in God and turn to prayer instead. Recalling her faith even enabled him to pray more. Yes, they were physically apart but they could still be united in prayer and that gave him a lot of comfort.

He brought himself to his feet and streamed along with the other passengers as they exited the plane into the airport. It took him an hour to pass through customs and immigration. Finally, when he arrived at the waiting area, he caught site of his uncle standing next to Adam. In that second he wished that Peace and Lawrence were there too. With his leather suitcase in one hand and a carryon in the other he negotiated his way through other travelers and approached his party. As soon as the doctor came close enough Adam stepped forward and relieved John's hand of the heavy suitcase. The driver had been witness to Mr. and Mrs. Ebem's separation from Peace and even though he restrained his conversation with John to a simple exchange of greetings, he felt a tremendous wave of sympathy for his boss's relative. He waited as uncle and nephew exchanged embraces. The elder man pulled back and studied his guest. He saw the eyes of a man in pain. The sight moved him but he would not speak of it, at least not in public.

"It is good to see you again," he said instead to his nephew.

"Yes, we had no problems on the way, thank God."

"How is your father?"

"He is doing very well on his own. He sends his greetings."

Without wasting another minute John asked, "Have you heard anything about Peace or Lawrence?" The question did not surprise his uncle.

Mr. Ebem shook his head. "I'm sorry. We know a journalist that was just there yesterday. We asked him to look for them. But he found that the whole village was deserted except for the Se fighters. They've taken over. Even our home is now a base for them."

John racked his brain for a moment. They had to have gone somewhere. They did not just vanish into thin air.

The men strode past an array of art shops bearing exquisite carvings, but John took no notice of them. Turning to his uncle he asked, "Isn't there a refugee camp or something like that?"

"Yes, there is a camp but it's across the border near the Carlma village."

Under his breath, John muttered the words, "Carlma village." Why did that name sound familiar to him? Within minutes, the *automatic sliding doors opened to usher them from the air conditioned structure into the night heat. Instinctively John freed himself from his leather fall jacket and flung it over his arm.*

At one o'clock in the morning they drove through quiet streets. The doctor sat next to his uncle in the back seat and remained deep in thoughts as they passed shop after shop. Once they passed an aging government building, he became once again aware of his surroundings. That's why the village of Carlma sounded so familiar. He recalled seeing it on the map when he came to the city to study the geography of his mother's village.

Turning away from the window to his uncle, he asked, "I suppose the quickest way to get there is to go through our village?"

"Get where?"

"To the camp at Carlma"

His uncle thought for a while. "You are right, but it is also the most dangerous. You will be better off flying into their capital and driving for about four hours to the camp."

The white car turned into a quiet street lined with palm trees. From his seat John looked over the black iron gates to the top of the two story house known as the Ebem's city residence. Adam pulled up before the gates and honked the horns. It took several beeps to summon the night watchman from the gatehouse. The stout man clothed in a brown t-shirt and a pair of khaki pants emerged from the gatehouse and yanked the gates open.

John wanted so much to get down to business and map out the details of his mission. First he needed to make a list of medications and first aid products that may come in handy. The doctor was fully aware of where he was headed, an area filled with traumatized and displaced people. There was a good chance that someone would need medical care. He had a great love for his mother's people. He would do anything in his power to help them.

Mrs. Ebem sprung from the living room couch at the barks of her Alsatian guard dogs. Quick steps brought her to the window. Moving aside her silk curtains she peered into the professionally landscaped front yard adorned with rows of flowering shrubs. With the other hand she shielded her eyes from the approaching vehicle's blinding headlights as it moved in the direction of the garages. She waited for the men to reach the house before leaving her spot by the window. With trembling hands she unlocked the front double doors.

"Welcome," she greeted in a voice filled with sympathy. Her arms embraced the doctor once he passed the threshold into the foyer. Then pulling back she examined his face. Mrs. Ebem noticed the same hurting look that her husband had observed earlier at the airport. The woman struggled for the appropriate words. If she said he looked well she would be lying. The circles under John eyes screamed lack of sleep. She exchanged glances with her

husband who stood behind John. He offered a helpless shrug.

She returned her attention to John. "Would you like a drink or something to eat?"

"No thanks. I'm alright." He stepped aside to make way for Adam who was busy moving a suitcase and a carryon bag into the foyer. Mrs. Ebem fumbled with her night scarf, she fought the urge to force him to eat something. They all thanked Adam for his work as he made his way out of the house to the one bedroom bungalow in the backyard. Aunt Florence waited until the door locks latched in place before addressing her nephew.

"You must be very tired then. We will let you get settled."

John nodded and picked up his things from the terrazzo floor. He was grateful to be left alone that night. His mind worked as he climbed each stair to the guest bedroom. Not bothering to unpack anything, he found a notepad and a pen and began to jot down items for his trip into an unknown land.

The next morning the young doctor rose with his relatives and attended the morning mass; a habit which God's grace enabled him to cultivate over the past months. He then returned home to a quick breakfast of toast and tea. Within minutes he was out again in his jeep. By midday John returned from various markets with bags containing first aid kits, medicine for malaria, a variety of antibiotics, rehydration drinks, pain medicine, boxes of latex gloves, towels, blankets and anything else his medical mind could think up. He also spent some time on the internet researching his intended destination. His plan was to leave for the airport in the morning.

That night, inside the guest room, he spent a good amount of time praying like never before. He asked God for guidance and for courage. Was he scared? Absolutely! He was about to step into unknown territory. But the woman he loved and her brother were nowhere to be found and his people were homeless. How could he not get on that plane?

CHAPTER 13

In the morning the high pitched sound of Mimi's voice asking us to wake up stirred me from sleep. She leaned against the doorway with both arms folded over her flower dress.

"Breakfast is getting cold," she said, her gaze moving back and forth between Charity and myself. I shut my eyes momentarily and offered my day to the Lord.

Charity let out a wide yawn. "Good morning," she greeted. "Have you seen Marcus?"

"He is outside speaking with our men." Our eyes followed Mimi's hand in the direction of the window. We saw Marcus sitting under a tree, surrounded by three other men. One of them possessed such a rich shade of grey hair that I guessed he just had to be the papa of the compound. Cock crows reached our ears followed by the laughter of playing children. It puzzled me that the little ones were not in school. I returned my attention to Mimi only to find the look of haste in her face. My question would have to wait for a more appropriate moment.

Mimi made for the door. "You will find water in the bathroom. Please hurry and come to the main house; we don't want the food to go to waste."

Just like Mimi had spoken, I arrived at the shower room to find a plastic jerrycan capable of holding about fifty gallons of water.

Clad in borrowed tie-die dresses and rubber slippers we exited the house an hour later into the brilliant sunshine. On our way to mama's house we stopped by the tree to greet the male members of the household. Marcus saw us approaching and rose to his feet from a carved round topped stool.

He took Charity's arm. "This is my wife," he explained to the men. "She has regained her strength and we have your household to thank for that." The men nodded in acknowledgment while Charity bent her knees momentarily in greeting.

"We are happy to help our brothers anyway we can," replied Papa. As I stood watching I noticed the unripe cashew fruits that hung from the tree branches. A bowl containing garden eggs and kola nuts sat at the center of the gathering which at the moment was of no interest to the men except for one of them. He looked the youngest, with a thick herd of hair and eyes filled with energy. The man finished the bitter tasting nut in his hand and helped himself to one of the eggplants.

I was content with my hidden position a few inches behind Charity until the grey haired man turned his gaze to me. He motioned for me to come forward. I obeyed, imitating Charity's method of greeting.

"I suppose this is your sister," he asked to Marcus.

"She is our very good friend."

"Where is your family?" prompted the older man to me, his eyes sparkling with interest.

"I lost them in the war."

A look of sympathy passed through Papa's face. "Sorry to hear that." Then almost immediately, he gestured to the man next to him who was still chewing.

"This is Samu, my youngest son." Papa smiled to reveal a struggling set of discolored teeth.

The younger man took a break from chewing his snack, "Welcome."

"Thank you," I replied. "My friends and I appreciate everything this household has done for us."

The next few moments entailed further introductions. We repeated our greeting gestures as the husbands of Mimi and Smallwife were identified to us

We eventually reached the main house where we consumed our cold porridge and joined the women in their housework which at the moment entailed processing fish. For hours we worked side by side removing scales, empting fish stomachs, washing their insides and cutting them to pieces. At the end of it all Smallwife and I seasoned and deep fried less than half of the catch while Charity and the other women smoked the remaining fish outside the house in the backyard. We must have processed over one hundred of them. The whole compound filled with the aroma of smoked fish mixed with wood smoke. Most of the dried fish would find its way to market and eventually into someone's soup pot.

When it seemed like our task was completed, I sat alone in the backyard of the main house. Charity had gone off to discuss something with her husband and the other women seemed occupied with their chores. I guessed from the heating temperature that it was midday. With folded arms I gazed upon an army of ants that filed their way across the sandy backyard to an unknown destination. Perhaps they were building a home nearby. I thought about our current situation. Our host family welcomed us with open arms but we could not stay and burden them forever. I knew that the time would come when we would need to move on from this family. *Jesus may Your Will be done.*

Without warning, one of Mimi's children emerged from the side of the house and ran up to me, panting and obviously seeking protection from someone or something. I quickly rose to my feet in anticipation of meeting the guilty party. The little girl clung to my side. She stood about three feet tall in a cream colored dress which was clearly too big for her.

"Don't let her get me!" she begged, her large eyes saturated with panic.

"What happened?"

"I spoilt Hope's slippers. I didn't mean to, I was just trying it on and now she is angry with me." Almost immediately Hope, a girl of about age seven, came running toward me with the broken footwear in one hand, her young eyes seeking vengeance.

She brought her bare feet to a stop right before me. "Aunty, Faith tore my slippers now I can't wear them anymore!" This was not the first time a non relative called me aunty. Many other children in our village had done the same. As a child, I was taught that it was disrespectful to address our elders by their first names. I supposed this village held the same views. To this young girl, aunty seemed like the best possible alternative. And frankly, I liked the sound of it.

I stretched out my hand to Hope. "Let me see the slipper."

Without hesitation she handed it over to me. To my relief the damage was minimal. One of the straps had managed to free itself from its socket but the strap remained intact.

In a gentle tone I addressed the younger child that still clung to my side. "Faith, are you sorry for what you have done?" With much eagerness she nodded.

"Tell your sister."

The little girl wasted no time in obeying, "I am sorry for spoiling your slipper."

My attention shifted to Hope. "It would be wonderful if you forgave your little sister."

Hope folded her arms together and shook her oval shaped head, her eyes watering by the minute. "I don't have anything else to wear."

I tried my best to sound as gentle as possible. "Hope, have you ever done something to offend anyone?"

Before she could answer Faith chimed in, "You knocked down Papa's bowl of rice before." This revelation caused the older girl to frown at her little sister.

"Is this true?" I asked to Hope.

She seemed embarrassed at being exposed. With reluctance she nodded.

"Did Papa forgive you?"

The girl moved her head in slow nods.

"How would you have felt if he had refused to forgive you?"

"Sad."

"You see why you should forgive your sister?"

"Yes," she answered. Then fixing her gaze on Faith she spoke the words, "I forgive you." A less frightened Faith let go of my dress and threw her arms around her sister. It was a moving sight. Why couldn't some adults reconcile just as quickly?

"Okay Faith," I began, "It's time to fix the slipper."

The little girl's face wrinkled with worry. "But I don't know how."

"I'll show you," I assured, patting her shoulder. "You still have a responsibility to fix what you have destroyed okay?"

"Okay."

Within minutes the girls walked away hand in hand as though their little conflict never existed.

"You handled that very well." I spun around to behold the girls' mother standing by the kitchen door. "Those two always have something to fight about."

"Do they attend school?"

Mimi shook her head with regret. "We cannot afford to pay their school fees. I try to teach them sometimes, but I am not very good at it. Maybe you can teach them for me."

"Of course," I answered. Refusing to help such an accepting family was not a possibility. In fact I was glad to be of use to them.

Mimi's sharp features produced a smile. "Very well, you can start tomorrow. I'll go and tell the girls." With that she scampered toward the front yard while I returned to our sleeping quarters for a nap.

Before the day's end we met once again at the main house for a fish and rice dinner. At bedtime Charity relayed her husband's findings to me.

"They want us to stay." Her eyes sparkled with delight. "Do you hear? We don't have to go to the camp." I smiled at Charity's excitement. Up until that moment I had no idea that she dreaded camp so much.

I sat up in my mattress and told her of my new teaching responsibility.

She squealed with delight. "They've also asked Marcus to go fishing with them. That means a bigger catch. And a bigger catch translates to a need for more helping hands, us! In return we get to stay here till the fighting is over."

For a reason unknown to me, I could not bring myself to share in Charity's level of excitement. Of course I felt gratitude for the chance to be useful and for the chance to live in a real home. But my heart remained with the people at camp. *Dear Jesus I abandon everything in Your hands. Thy Will be done.*

I woke up the next morning feeling well rested and ready to start teaching. Charity and I prayed together then we met the rest of the family at the main house for hot bowls of porridge. Afterwards, Charity accompanied the women to the market while I stayed behind to teach the girls. I decided that under the cashew tree was the best possible place to hold our lessons because of its shade and the outdoor fresh air.

A severed tree branch became my chalk and the sand my black board. I felt elated to find that both girls already knew their alphabets. This meant I could start teaching them how to read right away. On the first day they learned how to write their names. Their shrieks of excitement at seeing their own squiggly writings in the sand echoed throughout the yard. They spent the remainder of the day guarding the area from footprints so that they could show off the writings to their mother and father.

Watching the girls learn how to read and write new words proved to be a delight. As the days passed Charity, Marcus and I settled into our different roles within the family. The arrangement seemed successful. We continued to stay in the house intended for Samu and his future wife while the third son moved back into the main house with his parents.

On Sundays the family would lead us on a forty five minute walk to a convent where the locals gathered for mass. During mass we prayed for all and for those who had died. This village did not possess a parish of its own, but its citizens pulled together and gathered food for the people at camp. A bag of dried fish came from our hosts. Others contributed corn, rice, beans or whatever they could afford. Even though I had no material possessions to donate, my prayers went with the contributions. I also prayed for the time when we would all be able to return home.

CHAPTER 14

Nothing prepared Dr. Williams for the work awaiting him at the camp. A large field of patchy grassland formerly used to host soccer games and celebrations now served as hosts to hundreds of people, mostly women and children. Except for a few tents and makeshift shelters the majority of them had nothing over their heads to shelter them from the elements. As he searched for a suitable spot to park his vehicle, John marveled at the fact that the battered four door sedan actually carried him for four hours to this place. He had his doubts when he paid the owner the asking price equivalent to four hundred dollars, but the area lacked a car rental facility. The sedan might have been a 504 Peugeot at some point but years of reuse and repair had transformed it into a piece of metal with four wheels and an engine. The air conditioning quit years ago, peeled off paint obscured the original color and he soon discovered after purchasing the car that the driver side door would not open without a fight. Rather than waste precious time quibbling with the seller, he climbed in through the front passenger door and drove off in search of the ones dear to his heart.

He took little notice of the scenic views on either side of the road. Neither did he let a *mystery smell from the car seats bother him. The idea that he could be so close to finding Peace sharpened his determination to reach the camp as soon as possible. Gradually, the paved roads changed to a passage way comprising of potholes and ditches. He navigated those successfully only to find that all traces of asphalt eventually vanished leaving him in a narrow stretch of dirt with minimal road signs. Despite his map he stopped three times for directions. Hours later, his heart rate doubled at the sight of an aged sign bearing the words Carlma. John clasped the wheels tighter as he fought hard to contain himself. He needed to focus on navigating the treacherous roads otherwise he may not make it to camp at all. He made a mental note of the market entrance to his right and continued on his journey until he arrived at the football field.*

He stopped the car at the corner of a small clearing just before the elevated field. The first thing to grab his attention as he exited through the passenger door, that afternoon, was the distinct crying of a child. It soared above the sounds of people in conversation, women lamenting, and even the cries of other children. This cry of desperation tore at his heart. For that moment he postponed his search for Peace. In fast movements John pried open the trunk of the car and retrieved a small duffle bag containing diagnostic tools. He hurried toward the field, his eyes moving frantically through incomplete families huddled together in their little shelters. He passed several men and women as they worked together to build more shelters using sticks, stones and textile cloths.

Indistinct murmuring reached his ears as he stepped through sitting or lying forms. He was surprised at how many people recognized him from the village, but he could not stop to greet them. He followed the sound of the child's cries until he reached a spot on the ground where the widowed mother sat rocking her son in a failing attempt to calm her twelve month old. About a dozen people congregated near the mother. They had just completed a prayer for the suffering child.

John squatted next to the mother. At first she gaped at him in confusion. What was he doing here? Didn't he have a home away from the village? He unzipped the bag and clasped the stethoscope to his ears. Her nonplused look transformed to one of hope.

"I did not know you were a doctor." Instantly he heard the surrounding people repeating her surprised words.

He addressed the mother, "May I take a look at him?"

The woman lowered the boy from her clutch. The child's thin t-shirt and cloth diaper offered zero protection from biting insects. He ran his thumb over the bite marks on the child's legs. Then he pressed the stethoscope against the boy's chest, feeling appalled at the patient's temperature. There

131

were clear signs of an illness. He noted, among other signs, the dryness around the boy's lips and his sunken eyes. The poor child was also dehydrated. After listening to the boy's mother describe other symptoms he knew without a doubt that the culprit was malaria.

He packed his tools into the bag and rose to his feet. "I'll be right back." The mother nodded, her face saturated with gratitude. Within minutes the doctor returned with a small mesh bag containing a bottle of liquid medication, a medicine dispenser, four ounce bottles of a rehydration drink for children, and some granola bars. His other hand carried a pediatric scale. He weighed the child, and then he administered the first dose to the crying toddler, explaining each step to his mother. When John finished relaying the necessary information to her he advised the young mother to give the pediatric rehydration drink to her son. She obeyed, and in a short while the crying stopped. The boy rested his exhausted head on his mother's shoulder; he would fall asleep in no time. After watching the boy for a few minutes the doctor got the sense that this child would be alright.

He placed a hand on the mother's shoulder, "Your son should be fine. Keep persevering and eat something yourself," he said smiling.

She looked at him, her eyes shedding tears of gratitude, "May God bless you!"

"Thank you." Her words gave him more comfort than she could ever imagine. He

took her blessing seriously believing in his heart that it would come from Jesus Himself.

He gripped his bag in preparation for departure, "I am looking for a woman named Peace Udomm and her brother Lawrence. Do you know them?"

The widow shook her head. "I know them, but I don't know anything about their whereabouts." With an apologetic look she continued, "I will pray for you."

The doctor rose to his feet. "Thank you," he said, trying to hide his sorrow. "If you hear anything about them please let me know." With that he walked in the direction of his car. His shirt, drenched in sweat, clung to his back. As he moved past the villagers, his eyes still scanned the area for his fiancée and her brother. Several times he stopped and asked people about them. To his great disappointment nobody could tell him anything concerning their location. With fatigue setting in, he eventually climbed into his car and helped himself to a few gulps of water. Where could they be?

Before he could contemplate the question, another woman carrying a child about five years of age approached him. Again, he climbed out through the passenger door and waited for her. She must have followed him because his parking spot was not visible from the elevated field.

Upon her arrival she began to plead as though she feared being turned away, "Please forgive me for troubling you but I saw you help the other woman. My daughter has been sick for days."

The doctor took pity on her. He knew just by looking at her that she was weak.

"When was the last time you ate?" he asked.

The woman shrugged, "Two days ago. People said that some nuns from the village brought food this morning but we missed them. We only arrived a few minutes ago. They said the nuns promised to return."

Again the woman apologized, "Sorry to trouble you. I know you are looking for Peace. But can you help my child please?"

"Its no problem at all," he assured, shifting his gaze to the girl.

"How are you feeling," he asked softly.

The girl placed both hands on her temples. "My head hurts." He noted her distressed answer and proceeded to examine her just like he had done the twelve month old. This girl shared the same symptoms as the boy. As he returned to his trunk for treatment, his eyes caught sight of more women and children streaming down the grassy elevation toward him. Their large number seemed overwhelming. But deep down, he experienced gratitude at being able to serve such amazing, enduring people.

When he decided to start a clinic years ago it never occurred to him that it would be run from the trunk of a battered car. He saw patient after patient until the sun retired for the night. John continued to work with the aid of his uncle's solar powered night light. When he ran out of medication he still examined patients, jotting down his diagnosis, and their personal information such as names, ages, medical history or weights. A trip into town was in order.

Only after the departure of the last patient did John get a chance to process the day's events. One incident made an impression on him. A man in his forties came forward, hours earlier, with his sick son in his arms. After an examination of the five year old boy, John provided the medicine to treat the cause of the boy's fever. The man went away grateful only to return with a panicked expression in his tired face.

"I cannot give him the medicine." He reported to John. "I have tried different ways and each time he turns away with determination." From the tone in the man's voice John could see that the father was helpless.

"He is very ill," informed the doctor. "I will have to give him the treatment in the form of an injection."

An exhausted sigh left the man. Then with a tone of resignation he answered, "He hates injections, but I understand."

"I'm sorry," returned John. He really was. He wished there was something more he could do to make the situation more bearable for the boy and his father.

The boy remained motionless while John prepared the syringe. He rested in his father's arms until he felt the coldness of wet cotton balls on his skin. He let out a scream so strong that it was hard to believe that it came from such a weak boy. The doctor's eyes met the father's.

"He knows what is coming next," informed the father. Gently rubbing his son's back the man muttered the words, "Persevere, persevere."

"What's his name," asked John.

"Kenny," answered the father in a tired voice, "but we call him Junior."

"Okay Junior," began John in his gentle voice. "I need you to be still, okay?"

Tears streamed down little Kenny's cheeks. He shut his eyes as tightly as he could and clung tightly to his father who was still comforting him with so much paternal love and tenderness.

"The doctor will be done soon," he said softly to his son, "persevere."

With an intense focus on doing his job well, John administered the injection. A deafening yelp came from Junior. He buried his face in his daddy's chest.

Within seconds it was all over. It took Junior a while longer to stop crying. But the tension had passed. Even his cries reflected his relief as he rested his head on his father's chest.

Kenny Senior placed a kiss on his son's forehead. "When you begin to feel better you will see why you needed this injection," he said to his son who was gradually returning to a state of calm.

John's heart was touched at the sight of moisture in the father's eyes. The scene made John recall something which Peace had shared with him. She once told him that God stays with us in our times of suffering. John knew this to be true but he understood it better that day after watching the way in which Kenny Senior held his son tight, comforting him and strengthening him through the inevitable pain which was necessary to cure the boy. If an earthly father was capable of providing such strength and love as John had witnessed that evening, how much more our Heavenly Father Who is all powerful and loves us so much more?

The doctor checked his watch as cricket sounds ensued. Nine thirty five at night and he still hadn't found Peace. He settled into a passenger seat of the sedan. By far this was the longest day of his life. He felt tired but not as exhausted as when he first worked with Peace and Lawrence to harvest mangoes. John knew that his endurance improved considerably during the time that he spent with them. His former self would have collapsed after a day that began with a six o'clock morning flight, four hours on the road, more than a full day's worth of professional work and the clean up afterwards. Perhaps, all those days of farm work prepared him for his present circumstance.

His thoughts went to Peace. Despite his fatigue he spent some time in prayer for her and for the people in the field.

The people did their best under the circumstances; building their own shelters from things generally considered useless. Nothing was left to waste at the camp. John saw children build toys out of plastic scraps and marveled at their ingenious imaginations. However, the reality that they needed help remained. Would he be able to serve them and find his fiancée at the same time? Maybe the journalist was wrong. Perhaps Peace remained at home. He needed to talk to more people. There were approximately five hundred adults in that field. Someone had to have an answer.

He left the car, his strides moving quickly toward the camp grounds. The cream colored t-shirt worn by a young boy shone under the moonlight. He approached the teenager just before he crawled into his tent. The boy's youth made the doctor think of Lawrence.

"Excuse me"

The boy jumped at the sound of John's voice.

"I am looking for Peace or Lawrence Udomm. Do you know them?"

Without giving an answer the youth looked away.

Something about the youngster struck the doctor. He had seen that face before.

"What is your name?" he asked to the adolescent.

"Sam."

"Sam can you tell me anything about them?" The doctor's breath quickened for he sensed that this kid actually knew something.

Suddenly the youth burst out in tears. He fell to the ground and crouched in a fetal position. His cries attracted a handful of people. John moved closer and squatted next to him on the ground.

"Why are you crying?" he spoke gently.

With his hands over his face the boy answered, "I was there when Lawrence died. I knew all along that you were looking for them but I did not know how to tell you." Gasps came from several of the bystanders. One woman covered her face with her palms and walked away.

The doctor fought to maintain his composure. He felt as though another blow had just been delivered to his stomach. Lawrence was dead. A young boy of sixteen, misled to his death.

With his stomach turning the doctor asked, "Do you know anything about his sister?"

Still covering his face Sam answered, "They took his body to her, that's all I know." As John looked at the crying boy he began to realize where he had seen the youth before.

Sam was one of the boys that rode in the back of a pickup truck with Lawrence.

"Did you fight with him?"

The boy nodded, his cries intensifying. As much as John wanted to walk away and grieve alone, he stayed with Sam and tried to console him.

Later that night he sat alone in his sedan, his mind processing the new information. He found himself praying for Lawrence's soul and the soul of many others who had left the earth. Afterwards he considered what his fiancée must have suffered at seeing her brother's body. The thought brought tears to his face. Was she still alive? Only time would tell. He would have to keep looking. Deep down John understood that God was in control of everything. The doctor took comfort in the fact that Peace had a friendship with Jesus. The Lord would take care of her.

John hoped the nuns would return soon because he too needed lots of prayers. He still needed to locate his fiancée. Yet he could not leave his people. He felt a strong obligation to stay and care for the sick among his people, especially the little ones most susceptible to illness. He also needed to find real waterproof tents before the rainy season arrived.

It was a painful night. Several times tears came to his eyes at the thought of Peace burying her brother. He recalled the incident with little Junior and his father. John reminded himself that God was with him. Right there, in that car. Feeling a surge of hope, he clung to his Heavenly Father in prayer.

When daylight arrived he offered his day to the Lord and exited the mysterious vehicle. A good stretch coupled with the cool morning breeze helped relax his aching muscles. Before long he began his preparations for the day. Careful not to waste his rapidly depleting water he brushed his teeth and splashed some of the liquid in his face. A full day of work lay ahead of him. But first he wanted to check on his younger patients before leaving the camp for the market.

John approached the field to discover that most people were already awake at six o'clock in the morning. Some formed prayer groups while others worked to improve their surroundings. He walked through paths formed by rows of makeshift shelters while responding to several good mornings. The doctor found his first patient sleeping calmly in his mother's arms. The sight pleased John.

He turned to the grateful mother. "He looks better."

"Yes," she agreed, "I have been giving him the medicine as you directed.

A smile shone in his face. This was why he became a doctor. He could no longer imagine practicing his profession anywhere else. John moved on to check on a few others. He received satisfactory reports from each patient. He felt comfortable leaving for the market place. In a short while he reentered the Sedan and started the engine.

CHAPTER 15

The lone doctor returned from the market to find the biggest surprise of his life. After spending hours negotiating with traders over the price of tents, water, food and medicine, he arrived with a car trunk so heavy that the rear of his sedan sagged to the ground. Most of his money, including the amount donated by his relatives, was gone. But as he made the purchases to serve others he no longer felt the temptation to worry.

A handful of nuns dressed in white habits scattered throughout the field. To his delight they were not alone. A convoy comprising of one midsized bus and three trucks, each bearing the words Our Lady of Hope Missions, parked along the side of the road leading up to the field.

He brought his sedan to a stop behind the last truck. The doctor climbed out of the aged vehicle, his heart throbbing with excitement and approached the individual closest to him. She stood tall in her white ankle length habit, her hands clasped behind her as she surveyed an unoccupied section of grass near the trucks.

"Good day sister." His voice could hardly contain his excitement.

She looked up from her task. At the sight of him a smile drew across her fifty five year old face as though she was seeing an old friend.

The woman held out a slim hand for a handshake. "You must be the doctor we've been hearing so much about. I am Sister Florence."

John accepted the handshake. "John Williams. It's so good to see you all." Despite her double lens glasses he noticed the twinkle in her eye.

"You know," he began, suddenly feeling comfortable in her presence, "My aunt's name is Florence."

The sister smiled at the news. "I believe I know your aunt."

Her answer took John by surprise. He raised both eyebrows.

"Yes I do," continued Sister Florence. "Ever since we arrived this morning the people have done nothing but tell us all about you. They say you are related to Florence and Linus Ebem. I grew up with Florence you know. We attended the same secondary school. Years later we ran into each other in the university. She later married Linus while I went off to medical school. I haven't seen her since then."

With his arms akimbo John stood speechless, his mind digesting the news. "Does this mean you are a doctor?"

Sister Florence nodded, her features shifting in amusement.

"And you are not from Carlma then?"

She shook her head. "I was sent across the border to work in the city hospital over twenty years ago." Then motioning to the other nuns she continued, "When our fellow sisters living in this village informed us of the situation we left the city and came right away."

John let out a sigh of relief. "This is very good news. You have no idea how grateful I am to see you." Looking toward the field he asked, "Are there any other doctors?"

Florence shook her head. With a hand she waved away a housefly. "Just us and five nurses, but with God's help we will be fine."

Two men carried a huge folded tent past them. "Where do you want this?" The question came from one of the men.

Sister Florence waved her hands around where they stood. "We can setup right here." Returning her attention to John she added. "They are going to build our clinic."

A smile relaxed John's face. He joined the men in building the large white tent. When they were finished he looked at the result and thought of those event tents used for outdoor wedding receptions. As time passed he saw makeshift shower stalls spring up, another tent setup for food distribution and even a tent setup for the future school.

But the sight most pleasing to him was the fact that his people now had waterproof shelter over their heads. He helped the drivers unload cooking utensils, water, baby food, bags of grain and vegetables. When the men stopped for a break, John bowed his head and expressed his profound gratitude to God.

The next morning, before dawn, Samu left his room in the main house to search for his father. The youngest man in the household moved quietly through a dark hallway to the largest room in the house. He could not recall the last time he woke his father up from his sleep, but he deemed this disturbance necessary. The men had agreed not to fish the night before in anticipation of a celebration that was to take place that afternoon. Samu drew close to the plain wooden door. His knuckles delivered several raps loud enough to stir his parents. The older man came to the door, adjusting the traditional cloth that draped over his shoulder and sleeping trousers.

Seeing his son, the man left the room altogether and shut the door completely.

"Why are you up so early?" He asked to the young fisherman. Samu motioned for his dad to join him in the living room. Despite his tired muscles, Papa followed his son into an open space in the house. They settled across from each other on a woven mat.

"What is the meaning of this?" Papa asked again. "The cock has not even crowed yet."

Samu looked his father in the eye, "Remember what we discussed about Peace?"

The grey-haired man nodded, "Yes, you are going to ask her to marry you today. What is the problem?"

The young man hesitated. Papa saw this and mistook it for nerves.

"Don't tell me you are getting scared. When you see her in the yard, just walk up to her and talk to her. She is not going to bite you!"

"It's not that Papa."

Before Samu could say another word, his father interrupted again. "What is it then? Are you having doubts? Don't you see that she will make a very good wife and mother? I have watched her with those children. In fact, I knew from the moment we met her that our search for your future wife was over. We have been studying her, your mother and I. She is well behaved. Son, I assure you, you will be mistaken if you don't speak with her today."

Samu rubbed the back of his neck with his hand. He agreed with every word that came from his father's mouth. But he feared there was a problem, bigger than he could handle.

"Papa, I heard something yesterday."

Papa's eyes narrowed in confusion, "What? From where?"

"Some women from the market reported that a man came to them asking about Peace."

Silence filled the room. The news left Papa speechless. He looked away from his son through the window to the house where Peace slept.

"You mean our Peace?" Papa had allowed himself to grow fund of Peace. She was the daughter he never had. And until that moment he lived under the assumption that she would eventually marry his son and relieve Smallwife of her title.

Samu nodded. "He gave them her description and her last name."

"But that is impossible, she has no family."

"I don't think he is a relative," added Samu, *"The market women noticed that he spoke with a foreign accent."*

"If he is not a relative then what is he?" Papa's question hung in the air. Neither of them dared to voice their guesses.

The older man took a deep breath and blew into the air. "Where is the man now?" His tone suddenly grew weak.

"He told the women that they could find him at the camp."

The father mulled some ideas for a while, his gaze facing the window. "Go ahead and talk to her. We will have a meeting afterwards to decide how to proceed based on her reaction."

CHAPTER 16

"Camp! Why do you want to leave?" The moonlight, sneaking in through a gap in our curtain enabled me to see the shock in Charity's face.

I sat up in my mattress, taking care not to speak too loudly for fear of disturbing Marcus who was asleep in the living room. "I am not talking about leaving for good. I just feel that we should go to the camp and console our people. We have nothing physical to offer them but we can still bring them some comfort."

Charity thought for a while. Then with her gaze toward the floor she replied, "You have put me to shame. We've been here for a month and it never crossed my mind to go and see them."

"Do you want to come?" I asked.

She looked up at me, "Of course, but how will we get there? The sisters have to drive for an hour each time they visit camp."

"You have just given me an idea," I answered smiling. "We can ask the sisters to let us ride with them."

The following morning it was business as usual in our new residence. The bright sun warmed the soil. The children engaged in a game of hide and seek, and the family cock roamed about as usual only stopping to peck at some mysterious substance in the sand. The only thing that seemed out of place was the fact that the men did not go fishing the night before, but I soon dismissed it as nothing.

With so many women in the household, my chores seemed like nothing compared to my former duties at home. Besides helping with the fish, teaching the children and fetching water, there really was not that much to do. Mimi was so grateful at her children's progress that she would not let me do anything else around the house. I found myself with more free time than I was accustomed to. On that particular morning I sat alone in one of the stools under the cashew tree and pondered the best way to invite ourselves to visit camp with the sisters.

With my chin resting in my clasped hands, I fixed my gaze on the brown sand. My mind busied itself trying to recall the sitting capacity of the nuns' white van until an advancing shadow came into sight. I looked up to behold Samu walking toward me, his solid steps forming sandal prints in the soil. He came to a stop under the tree and settled into the stool next to mine. He sat with each arm resting on either knee and both hands clasped together.

"What is she thinking of this time?" He said the words with a hint of humor.

Despite his amusement I could sense the tension in his voice which also made me uncomfortable. Perhaps he wanted to be alone.

"Good morning," I greeted, rising to my feet.

The smile left his face. "Where are you going?"

"I'm getting out of your way. Don't you want to be alone under the shade?"

Shaking his head, he stretched out his hand and reached for my arm. "Stay, I want to talk to you."

I descended onto the stool, wondering what he could want to say to me. With my gaze returned to the soil I waited for him to speak.

He took a deep breath first, then in a firm tone he said, "I want to marry you." I almost lost my balance at this sudden proposal. Over the past month any conversation between Samu and I did not go past customary greetings.

Still refusing to look at him I asked, "Why would you want to do that? You don't know me."

My bewildered tone caused him to chuckle. "I know you better than you think. You have a kind disposition. You treat everybody with respect including my nieces and they are very fond of you. We know from what you have taught the girls that you care very much about what kind of people they will grow up to become. If you can take such good care of another's children, then you will know how to take care of yours."

I suddenly felt my temperature rise because I knew what my answer would be but I dreaded having to tell him. Samu was like a brother. I never once guessed that he would be interested in marrying me. If this village had the same traditions as we did, he would have already discussed his intentions with his family. They would all be waiting for an answer. Then it dawned on me. Was this why the men skipped fishing last night? I covered my face with both palms and thought about John. Tears came to my eyes.

"Look at me." He spoke with authority, though not threatening.

I obeyed, allowing him to see the tears and the look of regret in my face. With a slight shake of my head I gave my response, "I can't marry you. I'm sorry."

Even though he did not seem too surprised at my answer, his face betrayed the injuring effect of my response. With a sudden jerk of his head he turned his gaze in the opposite direction. He would not say a word. I rose to my feet and with one final apology I left him and hurried past Charity and Marcus to the privacy of our room.

Several minutes passed before the door opened to let Charity inside the small bedroom. With a look of sympathy, she sat next to my lying form on the mattress.

"Marcus just told me why they did not go fishing last night. I am sorry. I had no idea a marriage proposal was on the way."

"I couldn't say yes."

"Because of John"

I nodded, wiping the tears from my face. "Samu is like a brother to me."

"Well," said Charity, "He is twenty five years old. I'm sure he can handle rejection. Besides it is not your fault that you don't want to marry him."

My tear flows ceased gradually but I did not bother to lift my head from the pillow. "It is going to be awkward now, with us living in this house." I looked up at Charity who by now had moved to her own mattress. "You know, this is Samu's house. He will need it as soon as he finds a wife."

Charity's brows wrinkled with concern. After a few minutes of silence she decided, "I guess we may have to leave after all."

"Don't look so sad," I said. "We've been blessed with a roof over our heads and food to eat. It could have been worse. Besides he won't find a wife overnight."

Charity rose to her feet with an air of finality. "You are right, we have been blessed. Let us go to camp and comfort our people. We may be able to catch the sisters before they leave." She untied her scarf and retied it for a neater look.

I pushed myself up to sitting position. "You mean now?"

With a look of certainty she answered, "Yes, it is only seven o'clock if we go right now we can get there at seven forty five."

"But shouldn't we tell someone where we are going?"

"I'll tell Marcus."

I shifted uncomfortably in my bed. The idea of exiting the compound without speaking to the head of the household left me with an uneasy feeling. Before I could voice my concerns, Charity took a few steps toward the door then stopped. With critical eyes she examined me. "Please do something with your face. You look like you just woke up." With that she left the room to find her husband.

Taking Charity's advice I washed my face with soap and cold water. As I fastened on my white headscarf, I decided to stop and see Papa face to face. It would be hard but leaving without notice seemed rude, even if my intention was to return later that evening.

My companion was already in front of the house waiting for me. To my surprise Marcus also stood by her side. He donned a brown t-shirt, textile pants and a pair of rubber sandals. I closed the front door behind me, sensing that we had just gained another traveling companion.

"Marcus wants to come too," announced Charity taking a hold of her husband's arm.

I raised my shoulders, "Its no problem for me. I'll just go over to Papa's house and tell them that we are going out." I turned away from Samu's small bungalow and strode a few feet toward the biggest structure in the compound. Smallwife stood in front of the house with her arms folded before her. She looked like she had been expecting me to show up.

"Hello," I greeted as I walked past her to the entrance.

She placed a hand on my shoulder. And in her timid voice she explained, "They are having a meeting. No one is supposed to go in there." She grimaced apologetically.

I looked at her, "Every one is in there?"

She nodded, "Except for Mama and Mimi, they went on an errand."

"You can wait a while; maybe they will be finished soon."

I glanced around in search of Charity and Marcus only to find them advancing toward the compound entrance. Returning my gaze to Smallwife I answered, "I can't wait. We want to catch a lift with the sisters to camp. If I stay any longer we may not get to the convent on time." Pointing to the house I said, "Please tell them where we've gone. We hope to return this evening."

As I moved across the yard to join my travel companions I could not help but to wonder if the meeting had anything to do with Samu's proposal to me this morning. I quickly expelled the idea from my mind and hurried to catch up with my friends.

John stood outside his new tent and looked up toward the stars. Any observer would credit the sight above for the intensity of John's gaze but the real source of his seriousness was the struggle taking place in his mind. For the past two days he had spent every opportunity inquiring from people, both in the camp and in the marketplace, about Peace. So far his search seemed fruitless. Maybe she never really fled like the others. He shoved his hands in his trouser pockets and taking a deep breath, he blew into the night. With the presence of another full time doctor and a few nurses at camp, perhaps it was time to return to the home that Peace left behind and see for himself. Could she still be at the farm? The orchard with all those trees could serve as a hiding place, but not for long.

As much as he pondered the possibility of Peace never leaving, he always got the sense that staying at camp was the right thing to do. His adrenalin skyrocketed at the thought of her being in danger. John knew at once that it was time to pray. Without wasting another minute the doctor retreated into his tent and crouched down on the quilt where he clasped both hands together in prayer.

"Holy Mary mother of God please pray for her." He recalled the mother of Jesus in the Scriptures and how she prayed for others in the wedding feast at Cana, John 2:1-11. Jesus answered her prayers at that wedding on earth. Surely He would hear the Blessed Virgin Mary's prayers in Heaven for Peace.

The idea helped to return his heart rate back to normal.

He spent a few more minutes in prayer. Afterwards John stretched out on his back, his head resting on intertwined palms. Living in the unknown was not an easy ordeal to experience. What would he do without prayer? He surely would have lost it if it wasn't for God's Mercy. With these thoughts in mind he drifted off to sleep.

"It's Saturday. No school today!" The cries of two youngsters stirred John from his sleep. With one hand he shielded his eyes from the sunlight that filtered into his tent through a gap. The active winds beating against his shelter produced a flapping sound that reverberated throughout the canvas structure. Still in a lying position he brushed his face with one hand. He prayed his morning payers and sprung from his comforter. That Saturday was his day to work at the clinic.

CHAPTER 17

After nearly two hours of bumping through pot hole ridden streets, the white mission van carrying sixteen sisters, and the three of us arrived at the camp formally known as the celebration field. Except for pointed tent tops, there was not much to be seen from my spot in the front passenger seat.

Sister Grace, who had taken on the arduous task of steering the vehicle through bad roads exhaled in relief as she parked the van near the clinic.

"Thank God we are here," she said, the sweat still dripping from her temples. Her thanksgiving was echoed by sixteen other sisters. It was then that I realized the extent of the difficulties which they had to overcome just to get here.

"My friends and I are grateful that you have allowed us to come." I glanced toward the rear of the vehicle where Marcus and Charity sat. They also expressed their gratitude to the nuns closer to them.

"Hope you enjoyed the drive," answered Sister Grace, her small voice transforming to a chuckle. One by one we disembarked the van. Sister Grace led us across the grounds populated by dying grass to the entrance of a makeshift clinic. We observed a tall man dressed in a white shirt and khaki pants as he peered with an instrument into an infant's ear.

Could it be! This man looked so familiar! In that moment I opened my mouth to speak but could only deliver a gasp.

"He has fully recovered," said the man to the baby's mother who sat nearby in a folding chair.

"That's one of the doctors," whispered Grace to the three of us. Then scanning the surrounding area she continued, "I think this is his last patient for now. I'll introduce you in short while."

My hands began to tremble. It sounded just like John's voice, complete with that tone of kindness. The patient's mother, a young woman in her thirties looked past the doctor toward the entrance where we stood. Once our eyes met, she clasped a hand to her mouth and let out a gasp of her own. I recognized the woman whom most of us referred to as Paul's mother. She was one of my regular customers at our village marketplace.

The doctor, who stood with his back facing us, mistook her gasp for relief. "I can imagine how you feel," he continued. "It is a joy to see that your son is healthy again."

The woman did not answer him.

She jabbed a finger in my direction causing him to turn around.

At the sight of his face my breath fled from within me. I stood gaping at John, my legs threatening to give way. No one dared to say a word in that moment, not the sisters, not Charity, not Marcus.

He was really here! John was here with only a few feet between us! I wanted to scream out loud! I squinted as though that would make a difference to the sight before me. Charity's gaze went back and forth between us. I never dreamed I would once again behold this handsome face. He had not shaved for days, and his tired eyes limned lack of sleep. Surprising myself, I burst out in tears. He dashed towards me and held my teary face in his palms.

"It's okay," he said tenderly. "It's okay." For some reason his warmth and understanding caused me to weep even more.

"I'm sorry. I couldn't leave my brother," I said in between sobs.

"I understand," he whispered. "I completely understand. Thank God! Thank God for bringing you here!"

With her extra cloth, Paul's mother quickly fastened her baby on her back and hurried toward the field. Within seconds we heard her screaming at the top of her voice.

"Peace is here! Peace is here! The doctor has seen Peace!" Indistinct sounds of hundreds of people speaking at the same time traveled to us.

With moist eyes he looked at me.

"How are you?" Emotion loaded each word of his question.

"I'm very well, thank God!"

The voices from the field grew louder. John took my hand. "I suppose they would like to see you. They've been praying for you too." I nodded and we took our first steps away from the clinic. To our surprise scores and scores of people began to emerge from the elevation. They had already broken out in a cheer, the men and women dancing and singing to their rhythmic claps. I recognized Mrs. Afamu, the lead singer for our parish choir, as she belted out the impromptu lyrics for the occasion. She sang first then everyone else repeated after her.

"Praise be to God now and forever."
"Praise be to God now and forever."

"We will praise Him forever."
"We will praise Him forever."

"He has answered our prayers."
"He has answered our prayers."

"We will praise Him today, now and forever."
"We will praise Him today, now and forever."

"Our daughter has returned.
She is well and smiling."
"Our daughter is smiling, we will praise God forever..."

I looked up at John. He remained speechless; his watery eyes overcome with emotion.

The atmosphere rang with such joy and celebration that any passerby would think the conflict was over. The dancing women encircled us. And every once in a while someone would move through the dancers to the middle of the circle where John and I stood. I received embraces from many people, some of whom I did not even recognize. Along with the hugs came accounts of how much John had done to help them. Some told of how he spent hours walking through the camp in search of me. Even as I tried to dance along with the women, my person was moved beyond words because our people were not without troubles. And yet they were able to put aside their own concerns to pray on John's behalf. Before the celebrations ended, word spread throughout the camp that John and I were to be married.

EPILOGUE

I stood in our kitchen preparing dinner for my husband, my heart singing in thanksgiving to the Lord. It was the six month anniversary of our wedding. As I placed the onions on the chopping board my mind recalled the events that had transpired ever since that fateful day when John and I were reunited at the camp. Even though the government intervened to end the conflict, it took them two years to convince the Ses to return to their land. We came home to find the ruins of what was once my parent's house. But like many other villagers our hopes were not deterred as we fought daily to rebuild the lives that we once had.

We built our new home on the same parcel where the old one once stood. Budget requirements changed the plans from a two story house to a single level structure but it turned out to be the most beautiful home I had ever seen. From John, I learned a great deal about solar power. Since our climate was blessed with abundant sunlight, it only made sense that we should install the solar electric system in our home. The decision to do this meant sacrificing the second level of our house but it also meant that we would never have to endure the noise of the generator engine or stand in line to purchase its fuel. The house consists of a real kitchen with only the necessary appliances. We agreed to do without the dishwasher. Four bedrooms and two bathrooms occupied the left of the twenty five hundred square feet structure. On the right sat the living room, kitchen and John's study.

I finished slicing the onions and placed them in a pan of hot oil. The crackling sound dominated the room, but that did not stop me from thinking of the second time I had to separate from John. It was difficult. While John remained at camp he made arrangements for me to return to his uncle and aunt. Despite the tears we agreed that it was for the best. I was to study nursing while living with the Ebems so that I could be of assistance to John when the time came for him to return home and start our clinic. After watching the nuns care for our sick with such love, I knew without a doubt that I needed to become a nurse. For two years John remained at Carlma while I obtained the necessary qualifications that would enable me to serve our people alongside John.

Soon after his return from camp, we embarked on the necessary marriage preparation steps provided by our beloved Church to her children. In order to avoid grave sin, John did not move into the Ebem's residence where I was staying. Instead he stayed with one of their sons. From his cousin's residence he traveled often to the village to oversee the construction of our home and the clinic. The clinic though not fully completed is already in use. Our patients receive care from a one room structure while the builders work to complete the other buildings.

Feeling satisfied with the texture and aroma of the sautéed onions, I added the diced plantains, John's favorite. In a short while the ground crawfish and diced tomatoes would go in. A smile inched its way to my face as I recalled the moment when John and I stood before the altar of God and received the Sacrament of Marriage. It was six months ago. When John said the vows I knew that he meant every word. Our experiences from the war gave us a new appreciation for every moment that we breathe. Jesus stayed with us during all those days of conflict, providing us with the necessary strength and people to help us face each day.

I thought of the kind family at Carlma. I will never forget their kindness on that day when we emerged from the bush with pleading eyes. We were helpless and they took us in, sharing the little they had with us. Recently, Smallwife sent a message to Charity informing her that she no longer had to bear that title. Samu married from a family that lived only fifteen minutes away from them. Mimi began teaching her daughters after my departure. Her efforts enabled the girls to become fluent readers. We also learned the topic of Samu's family meeting which took place on the day that Charity, Marcus and I left to visit camp. They were discussing the best way to ensure that John was not a threat to my safety. They wanted to clear up that question before taking me to see him.

When the plantains browned, I added the remaining ingredients and turned the heat to low. In that moment I glanced through the window to behold the setting sun. I could hear the faint sounds of Charity and Marcus's sons playing in their yard. The laughter of their two children always brought joy to my heart. I chuckled, moving away from the stove to the fridge for a glass of water.

Within minutes, dinner was ready. I washed three of the mangoes from our orchard. Sam, the young boy that witnessed Lawrence's death came home to find that his parents and siblings died while he was fighting. Even though he lives with a distant cousin, we allow him to harvest our produce and sell them for his own profit. Since Sam is unable to complete the harvest by himself he sometimes contracts other youngsters to help out. They split the profits and he brings us a basket to show his appreciation.

I strolled to the living room where I spent some time in prayer for the faithful departed, especially the forgotten souls and those of my family. Thirty minutes later I left our living room couch to set the table. Just like clockwork the sound of John's jeep entering our compound reached my ears.

With renewed giddiness, I brought the jug of water to the table and rushed to the door. This is what I loved the most about being able to reach the house before John. I got to welcome him home everyday! My day at the clinic ended at five o' clock in the evening. But John always stayed behind for an hour to update his notes and records.

I opened the door while he was still searching for his keys. I couldn't help the huge grin that permeated my face.

"What's all the excitement about?" he asked as he planted a kiss on my forehead. A smile already animated his face even before I had said anything to him. That was my John, so willing to share in my joys and sorrows.

I took his hand and led him to the dining room where the table was set for three. "Our dinner is ready."

He immediately noticed the extra plate and asked, "Are we expecting someone?"

With giddiness I returned, "Yes a very special someone."

He glanced at his watch. "What time is this guest due?"

Right then I took his hand and revealed the news. "She is expected to arrive in nine months and when this special person does she will not be a guest. She will have our last name." At this point I knew my eyes gleamed in excitement. We both have waited for this time ever since we got married. We prayed and prayed, and now our dear God has answered our prayers and blessed us with a child. For a moment a puzzled look passed through his face, and then he understood.

"Hey, why do you keep referring to our baby as a she?" he asked in mock complaint. We laughed and rejoiced and thanked God for His many blessings, for the blessing of this special person growing within me, a person who's life is so precious that it can never be replaced by another.

Printed in the United States
79761LV00005B/13-18

9 780979 225819